He'd already asked the nurse a hundred questions.

He hadn't sat down.

He'd asked if there were information booklets he could read, Internet sites he could look up, doctors he could talk to—as if their baby's health and survival depended on him knowing everything there was to know about state-of-the-art preemie treatment, the way his business success depended on him knowing everything about a particular company or market.

It grated on Reba's red raw nerves, and she wanted to yell at Lucas, "How is this going to help? Is this what our daughter really needs from you?"

But nobody yelled at the NICU, and she wouldn't yell at the father of her baby, who was *here*, when she hadn't had a clue, eight hours ago, just how much she would need him.

And just how close to him she would feel.

Dear Reader,

Get ready to counter the unpredictable weather outside with a lot of reading *inside*. And at Silhouette Special Edition we're happy to start you off with *Prescription: Love* by Pamela Toth, the next in our MONTANA MAVERICKS: GOLD RUSH GROOMS continuity. When a visiting medical resident—a gorgeous California girl—winds up assigned to Thunder Canyon General Hospital, she thinks of it as a temporary detour—until she meets the town's most eligible doctor! He soon has her thinking about settling down—permanently....

Crystal Green's *A Tycoon in Texas*, the next in THE FORTUNES OF TEXAS: REUNION continuity, features a workaholic businesswoman whose concentration is suddenly shaken by her devastatingly handsome new boss. Reader favorite Marie Ferrarella begins a new miniseries, THE CAMEO—about a necklace with special romantic powers—with *Because a Husband Is Forever*, in which a talk show hostess is coerced into taking on a bodyguard. Only, she had no idea he'd take his job title literally! In *Their Baby Miracle* by Lilian Darcy, a couple who'd called it quits months ago is brought back together by the premature birth of their child. Patricia Kay's *You've Got Game*, next in her miniseries THE HATHAWAYS OF MORGAN CREEK, gives us a couple who are constantly at each other's throats in real life—but their online relationship is another story altogether. And in *Picking Up the Pieces* by Barbara Gale, a world-famous journalist and a former top model risk scandal by following their hearts instead of their heads....

Enjoy them all, and please come back next month for six sensational romances, all from Silhouette Special Edition!

All the best,

Gail Chasan
Senior Editor

Please address questions and book requests to:
Silhouette Reader Service
U.S.: 3010 Walden Ave., P.O. Box 1325, Buffalo, NY 14269
Canadian: P.O. Box 609, Fort Erie, Ont. L2A 5X3

THEIR BABY MIRACLE

LILIAN DARCY

SPECIAL EDITION®

Published by Silhouette Books

America's Publisher of Contemporary Romance

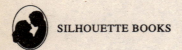 SILHOUETTE BOOKS

ISBN 0-373-24672-2

THEIR BABY MIRACLE

Copyright © 2005 by Lilian Darcy

Visit Silhouette Books at www.eHarlequin.com

Printed in U.S.A.

LILIAN DARCY

has written over fifty books for Silhouette Romance, Special Edition and Harlequin Medical Romance (Prescription Romance). Her first book for Silhouette appeared on the Waldenbooks Series Romance Best-sellers list, and she's hoping readers go on responding strongly to her work. Happily married with four active children and a very patient cat, she enjoys keeping busy and could probably fill several more lifetimes with the things she likes to do—including cooking, gardening, quilting, drawing and traveling. She currently lives in Australia but travels to the United States as often as possible to visit family. Lilian loves to hear from readers. You can write to her at P.O. Box 381, Hackensack NJ 07602 or e-mail her at lildarcy@austarmetro.com.au.

Chapter One

March in Biggins, Wyoming was cold.

Lucas could feel the threat of snow hanging in the air as he climbed out of the top-of-the-range SUV his father had bought late last year for tooling around the Halliday Corporation's newest ranch. Across the street, the Longhorn Steakhouse beckoned warm and bright, and he ignored his uncharacteristic hesitation about going in.

Reba Grant would probably be there, working the big grill in the kitchen, behind the swing doors. He'd come here in the hope of seeing her—*needing* to see her, somehow—but that didn't mean he looked forward to it. He knew it was likely to be a prickly and emotional meeting, uncomfortable for both of them.

Pushing open the door, he was greeted by warm air that smelled of good food and fresh coffee, and by Friday night crowds that might camouflage his arrival for a little longer, if he wanted more time. A red-haired waitress showed him to a small table in the corner. She moved with harried efficiency, snapping a menu in front of him, and asking if he wanted something to drink.

"Just water, thanks."

"Coming right up."

Her smile was short and small and landed somewhere over his left shoulder because she'd already turned away, which was just the way Reba had smiled at him the last time they'd met face to face, just before Christmas. They'd only had a short conversation, and it had felt awkward. He'd sensed her hostility. About a week after that, he'd seen her here in town and he was ninety-five percent sure that she'd seen him, too, but she'd quickly crossed the street and disappeared into the hardware store and they hadn't talked.

No, he didn't want more time.

They needed to talk tonight.

Having spent most of the past two and a half months at his home base in New York working fifteen-hour days on Halliday corporate business, Lucas had been slow to reach this decision, but he was right on top of it now.

They definitely needed to talk.

Reba had no right to feel hostile, but apparently she did, and that could surely only mean one thing. She had no idea how much Lucas had shared her own grief for what they'd lost in November.

He needed to tell her about his grief, here on her own territory, and they both needed to achieve some kind of closure and a way to handle the casual dealings they might occasionally need to have with each other in the future, now that he planned to spend more time at Seven Mile Ranch.

Hang on, *casual* dealings?

He questioned this word choice as soon as it flipped into his mind.

There had never been anything casual about Reba Grant, and it wasn't a word people often applied to Lucas himself, either. There certainly hadn't been anything casual about the way they'd first connected six months ago, back in September. Just because neither of them had wanted or envisaged—or had had the courage and imagination to consider, was that it?—a future to their immediate attraction, that didn't mean it had been casual.

He looked at the waitress again, at her full tables and her waiting clientele. She had a strong, compact build, must only be in her late twenties—around Reba's age— and seemed to have no trouble handling the workload. Just before the smile, she had thrown him a curious glance that suggested she knew exactly who he was, but still she would probably be a while getting back to him, the Halliday name notwithstanding.

If Reba was working tonight, she would be run off her feet, too. Maybe he should wait before seeking her out, but he didn't want to. He'd only flown in from New York this afternoon, and he wanted to get this issue tabled and dealt with as soon as possible.

He mentally decided on his order and watched the waitress disappear through the swing door to the kitchen, taking another table's empty plates. With one elbow, she held it open for a second waitress, heading in the opposite direction. He glimpsed the choreographed chaos centered around the grill and the fryer, and yes, there was Reba's back view. He recognized it easily—the odd combination of grace and toughness in the way she held herself, the glossy mass of her dark hair.

Remembered desire flooded him like a tide.

Remembered fulfilment, too.

He knew how wildly that body moved in ecstasy. He remembered the creamy color and silky texture of her skin beneath her clothes, as if he'd seen and touched her yesterday. He knew the way her hair smelled, so simple and fragrant and good, and the throaty sound of her laugh.

Yes, that was definitely Reba.

Then, as the door swung closed again, she half-turned in order to reach for something, and for a moment he almost thought...

No.

Impossible.

But he kept watching the door, and he stood up at his table, to get a better view.

The door opened again within seconds, and this time what he saw left him in no doubt.

Reba was pregnant.

Still.

When he'd believed until this moment that she'd lost their baby in a miscarriage during her first trimester late last year.

"Somebody wants to talk to you," Reba heard, but hardly took in which of the waitresses was speaking—definitely not Carla—because the woman had already disappeared again, carrying a pile of plates.

She looked up from the grill, and Lucas Halliday stood there, turned to stone just as she'd known he would, the moment they encountered each other again. He had the same instant, powerful effect on her senses that she remembered with an intensity that was almost like pain, and deep down this didn't surprise her, either.

He looked every bit as angry as she'd expected, too, although she would challenge his right to feel that way, with all the energy she could muster.

"This isn't a good time, Lucas," she said, steady-voiced.

"From your perspective, maybe. From mine, it's a very good time." He shot a cold glance down at her bulging stomach. "You have a hell of a lot of explaining to do, Reba, overdue since we saw each other before Christmas, and I don't see why I should wait any longer."

"We're run off our feet." Her body had been telling her so for an hour or more. Her stomach ached below the hard, rounded jut of her growing pregnancy. It was a dull sort of ache that tightened around her like an uncomfortable belt then eased, which meant that she forgot about it as she worked, then remembered it when it came again.

"Take a break, Reba." Her best friend Carla suddenly appeared, and touched her arm with a concerned gesture. She must already have seen that Lucas was here and she'd been hovering, waiting to step in when Reba needed her.

The two of them had known each other since school. Carla worked here as a waitress, and she had two children, one of them still a baby. Had she felt this same nagging ache at this point during her pregnancies? Both times, she'd worked until just a couple of weeks before the babies were due, but she'd never mentioned any problems or pains.

"I'm not scheduled for a break," Reba answered her friend.

Carla took no notice. "You need to talk to him," she said in a low voice. "Might as well make it now. The guy looks as if he can't decide whether to faint or punch a wall."

"Carla…"

Lucas was still standing there, stony and angry and shocked, ready to erupt as soon as he could get her alone.

"Twice you've thought it was over between the two of

you, right?" Carla muttered. "Once in September, by mutual agreement, then again when you miscarried the twin in November. You have a history with him, Reba."

"And a future, too." Reba closed her eyes. Some kind of future, good or bad. He was the father of this baby, and it was already clear to her that he wasn't going to let the issue go. "Okay, Carla, I know."

"Gordie not in tonight, Reba?" The steakhouse's newest waitress slipped by and threw the cheerful, familiar question at her, apparently oblivious to a tension in the air that had nothing to do with Gordie McConnell. Reba's long relationship with Gordie had been over for more than eight months, although Gordie and half of Biggins didn't seem to have gotten this straight in their heads, yet.

Reba gritted her teeth. "Haven't seen him, Dee," she answered.

Carla hissed in her ear, "Go. Now. Manager's office. Your place, even. Talk to Lucas. Before Gordie does show up and make this even harder." She stole the metal steak flipper out of Reba's hand and pushed her toward the swing door. "Someone else can cover for you."

"I have a table in the corner," Lucas offered, his voice cold and his body wound tight.

"No. I'm not talking about this here, in front of half of Biggins," Reba answered him. "We'll go into the manager's office, like Carla suggested." She began to move in that direction at once, and he followed her, practically breathing down her neck.

"I'm glad you appreciate that we have some talking to do," he said.

"It would be a little pointless to deny it, at this stage."

"But you were planning to, if I hadn't shown up."

"No, I guess I knew you'd have to find out eventually.

I was hoping it wouldn't be until after the baby was born. And I should make it clear to you, Lucas, I don't consider that you're involved."

"How in hell can I not be involved? Is this why you were so cool before Christmas? You were afraid I'd guess?"

"No. I didn't know, then. I was angry, and I had good reason to be."

But he'd focused on her first words, not her claim about anger. "You didn't know? That doesn't make sense."

"It will in a minute." She opened the manager's office.

"Good, because I'm keen to hear," he drawled, his voice as hard as whetstone. He entered the cramped office behind her and shut the door with a snap. The noise level from the restaurant fell away. "What I'm seeing is impossible. So start from the beginning. Tell me how in hell you staged that scene at the restaurant in Cheyenne, and at the hospital. Never mind my untrained eye, how did you convince a doctor that you'd lost the baby?"

She shook her head. "I can't believe you think I'd do that."

"I wouldn't, without the evidence. But I tend to trust facts, not feelings."

"I never staged anything, Lucas." She turned to face him, feeling that strange and almost painful belt-tightening feeling again, around her stomach and across her back. As usual, it soon faded. Her desire for a comfortable chair and a pillow to support her lower spine remained, destined to stay unfulfilled.

With its littered desk and single chair, the office was way too cluttered for this confrontation, but she was glad she'd chosen privacy over space, all the same. Lucas Halliday still looked too good, in her eyes, still filled her with all the wildly contrasting feelings he'd generated in her almost six months ago, and again in November. Anger and resentment, unwilling interest in just what made him tick, steaming attraction, dawning respect.

"And that's not the beginning, anyhow, and you know it," she finished.

"So start with your definition of the beginning," he said. "That first afternoon in the cabin? The night we tried to say good-bye at the door of my motel room? The day you came to see me out at the ranch in November?"

"None of those times."

"No, I guess not. I guess it goes farther back, doesn't it?"

Their eyes locked together. His looked dark and clouded with multiple layers of memory, and she knew he would have to define "the beginning" the same way as she did—the day, last September, when they'd first met…

Chapter Two

Lucas Halliday had no problem with buying a ranch for his father. He'd already bought four of them, over the past two years. All four had proved good investments, with his own regular visits to oversee things, and with the right people in place to run them.

This new purchase, however, was different. Dad's latest wife—the third since his long-ago divorce from Lucas's mother—had developed a very pretty fantasy about buying a real cattle ranch to use as a fourth home. Fifth, if you counted the yacht.

Raine wanted watercolor mountain views, a *Vogue Living* log cabin, movie soundtrack mooing steers—odorless, naturally—and a Fountain of Youth fishing stream. Dad was happy to go along with all of that, as long as the ranch paid its own way, just like the others did.

Lucas had been tasked with locating this impossible

combination. He'd narrowed the search to southern Wyoming, because of its relative proximity to Colorado ski resorts and the airline hub city of Denver, and eliminated two properties, sight unseen. If he couldn't give Dad and Raine a good report on Seven Mile he planned to tell them they could continue the quest on their own. He preferred cool-headed corporate takeovers to fantasy fulfilment for spoiled stepmothers, any day.

Having told the realtor that he would need three days to look over the place properly, he intended to be out of Wyoming and on a plane back to New York within half a day if Seven Mile fell short of Broadbent's glowing description.

He got into Denver on a late flight, rented a car, drove north through Fort Collins to Laramie to get a better impression of the region, then southwest to Biggins. By the time he'd checked into the town's best motel and eaten a late and surprisingly good meal in the quietest corner of the Longhorn Steakhouse, he was pretty convinced he'd be heading out of here tomorrow.

Biggins had no clothing boutiques, and no craft galleries or antique stores. There were just three motels, two options for dining and a single beauty salon. Raine expected big city amenities at a stone's throw from rural beauty, but she wasn't going to get that here.

Jim Broadbent knocked on Lucas's motel room door at eight-thirty the next morning, and they drove out to Seven Mile together. It was a pretty drive. The Medicine Bow Range dreamed in the distance. Rolling grasslands filled the foreground. The September grass was colored in the morning light like yellow chalk and fresh honey and clear-varnished pine floors.

Jim kept his conversation down to an intermittent trickle of facts about cattle breeds, growing seasons and water rights. An experienced realtor in his early fifties, the man gave the impression that he wouldn't find this ranch too tough to sell, even in the unlikely event that Halliday Continental Holdings didn't want it. He probably conveyed this same impression with every property he handled, and Lucas ignored it completely.

The mountains got closer. They passed the entrance to another property, and he had time to glimpse the name McConnell on the gate. Jim crossed a wide, shallow stream where the water ran silver over the rocks. Lucas knew that whatever attributes and advantages the Seven Mile Ranch might or might not have, it was going to be beautiful.

They turned onto a dirt road, and rumbled across several cattle guards. Ahead he saw a cluster of corrals and farm buildings, neat and modest and well-maintained. From this angle, they were almost lost beneath the enormous, soaring sky and looming mountain range.

"Who's giving me the tour?" he asked Jim, as they approached the long, low ranch house, painted a faded barn red. "You?"

"I'm going to leave you with Joe Grant. Or his daughter." Broadbent swung around and parked in the front yard at a crooked angle, then added, "Looks like it's the daughter. Rebecca. Reba, everyone calls her."

Rebecca Grant must have been sitting on the porch steps, waiting for their arrival. When Lucas caught sight of her emerging from the morning shadow cast by the house, she was still slapping her hands back and forth across the butt of her jeans to get rid of the dust.

She hadn't dressed to impress, he noted, as her body hit the sun. Old Wranglers, scuffed boots, plaid flannel shirt. A swathe of dark hair hung around her face and partway down her back, glossy and healthy and natural.

As Lucas watched, she dragged a red circle of elastic from her pocket and pulled the mass of hair into a high ponytail at the back. The movement lifted her breasts inside the rumpled shirt and showed a glimpse of shadow on soft skin. She'd just completed the final twist of the elastic when she reached them.

"Hi," she said. A wide smile jerked tight on her face and faded too soon. Mistrustful, ocean-toned eyes glinted like water.

"Reba," answered Jim. "Beautiful morning."

The realtor made introductions, and Reba chopped a hand in Lucas's direction for him to shake. He complied, and felt the startling contrast of long, fine-boned feminine fingers and palms callused like cardboard.

"Is your Dad around?" Jim asked.

"He's taken Mom into Cheyenne."

"Doctor?"

She nodded, but didn't say anything further on the subject.

"So you have a program mapped out for Mr. Halliday?"

"I thought we'd focus on the business side of the ranch today. The infrastructure. We'll look at the recreational amenities tomorrow, Mr. Halliday, if you're still interested in the place. We can take a drive down to Steamboat Springs, tour the far boundaries of the property. There's a little cabin higher up, and you can get an idea of the fishing and gaming possibilities. If you're still here after all that, we'll take a closer look at the cattle."

"Sounds good."

"For now, we'll start with the house," she said, "since Mom's not here to get disturbed by us coming through. Then the corrals, machinery sheds."

"Forget about the house," Lucas said, thinking aloud— insofar as he was thinking at all. Raine would be unimpressed with the ranch's primary residence. She'd want it bulldozed to make way for something much grander. "It'll have to come down, anyhow."

Rebecca flinched and pressed her lips together, making her chin jut, and he realized that his statement had been cruel. She'd probably called this place home her whole life.

He couldn't imagine what that would be like. Since his parents' divorce when he was three, his mother had lived in four different homes, and his serially divorced and remarried father in…he'd lost count. At least seven. Lucas himself had shuttled back and forth between most of these so-called homes until going away to college at eighteen, but he'd never put down roots in any of them.

At one level, it had been fun, and yet… A faintly remembered sense of bewilderment and loss blew over his spirit, and for a few moments he almost envied Rebecca Grant.

Neck and jaw muscles tight with regret, he considered an apology, but that would only make his mistake worse. He wasn't used to this kind of situation. His purchases and his takeovers didn't usually have the power to hurt someone like this, on a personal, individual level.

The meaning of her jerky smile, mistrustful eyes and abrupt handshake became clear to him.

She didn't want to sell.

"Would you like to stop in for coffee before we start, Jim?" Reba asked the realtor, but he shook his head. He was anxious to get out from under the awkward weight of atmosphere, probably.

"You'll drop Mr. Halliday back to town when he's ready, Reba?"

"Or Dad will." Her voice was a little husky, and deeper

than Lucas would have expected. It seemed to curl around him like a ribbon of scented smoke, drawing him in.

I should have driven the rental, he decided. Instead he'd listened to Jim's warnings about dirt roads and confusing directions. Now he was beholden to prickly, intriguing Reba Grant in a way he didn't like.

"Lucas, you're going to be real impressed with this place."

Jim offered the comment as he climbed into his vehicle. He roared out of the yard and back along the dirt track to the main road while Lucas was still, uncharacteristically, searching for the right reply. He really had no desire to hurt this woman, after the unthinking body blow he'd already delivered.

"Well, *I'd* like coffee," she said, on a slow, stubborn drawl.

She turned on her heel and stalked toward the house, like a bad-tempered horse. Compared with the women he was used to, she didn't walk with grace. Her movements were too angular, and too purposeful—blunt body language, surprisingly expressive.

Attractive, even.

Behind her, Lucas kept watching, for longer than he should.

"Sounds good," he told her.

"So you'll have to waste time on the house, after all," she said sarcastically, over her shoulder.

"Listen, Ms. Grant—"

"You probably have no idea how it feels to care about a place like this, right?"

"No, you're right, I don't," he answered, his voice clipped and tight.

"You probably think it's only possible to care about a home with sixteen rooms and fifteen foot ceilings and priceless artwork on the walls."

"Actually there's no home I care about in that way."

She stopped, turned fully, and stared at him for a moment. He stared back with narrowed eyes, masking the unexpected vulnerability he felt.

"Oh, well." She sounded less defiant now, and her eyes had softened a little, although the words themselves were still an attack. "Maybe over your coffee you can work out the best angle for the wrecking ball, or something."

He didn't trouble to tell her that using a wrecking ball on this place would be like using a stonemason's hammer on a thumb tack. In fact, they needn't 'doze it at all. They could haul it to some less desirable position and use it as a bunkhouse for ranch hands or for the house staff Dad and Raine would require when they were in residence.

Yep, definitely. Ideal. Practical. Inexpensive—it would come right off its footings, and onto a truck. There was no basement.

Would moving it instead of wrecking it come as good news to Reba, after his initial blunt announcement? Lucas didn't think so, somehow. This house looked as if it had grown in this spot, like lichen on a rock. She wouldn't want it moved.

Ahead of him, she reached the screen door. It opened into a screened-in porch that ran across the house's narrow front and around to the side. Her backside rocked as she pushed on the door and stepped inside, and he had to pull his gaze away.

There was something about her. You couldn't call her pretty. And "beautiful" was such a loaded word. All the women he knew were beautiful. It didn't fit her, either. But she definitely had something. A current of energy running in her veins, a kind of magnetism, and undeniable strength.

Whatever report he gave his father about this place in the end, he knew he wasn't going to be bored here today.

Rebecca led him into a big farm kitchen and he saw furniture comfortably worn from use, and huge windows showcasing views of the mountains. On the bench top, a coffeemaker sent out the aroma of ground beans steeped in boiling water. She slung the dark liquid into two mugs like a waitress. She didn't ask him if he wanted cream or sugar, just raised the waxed carton, the china bowl and her eyebrows.

He shook his head. "Black, thanks."

Was it his imagination, or did she add generous quantities of both cream and sugar to her own mug with a big dollop of attitude at the same time?

"There you go," Reba said, as she slid the steaming beverage in Lucas Halliday's direction.

She was glad Mom and Dad weren't here. She squeezed another token smile onto her face, then let it drop as soon as it had fulfilled its contractual obligations. She didn't want to sell this place.

If it wasn't for her mother's health, and the much easier life Mom would have down in Florida where her sister lived, it wouldn't be happening. And if Reba hadn't broken off her long-standing engagement to her ranching neighbor Gordie McConnell two months ago, it wouldn't be happening, either. She and Gordie could have run the two ranches together, leaving Mom and Dad free to make their move, but she didn't have the right skills to do it on her own.

She had known that showing potential buyers around her home would be hard, and she'd dreaded it, but the reality was even harder.

The reality was Lucas Halliday, corporate wheeler-dealer, heir to the family empire, dressed down in elastic-sided boots, jeans just old enough to fit right and a thin cotton sweater with a designer label subtly emblazoned on the left breast pocket.

He unsettled her. The way he moved, like a man accustomed to his road through life paying out as smooth as ribbon in front of him. The way he looked.

He wasn't conventionally handsome. His top lip was fuller than the lower one, and his prominent cheekbones were slightly uneven. His nose had a bend in it, just below the bridge. His skin was a little rough, as if he'd had trouble with it in his teens. But he had amber brown eyes, a strong chin, hair the color of maple syrup with a handful of Atlantic sand tossed in and a body that could have sold gym equipment to any man in America.

Let him buy the ranch, if he wanted it. She hoped he would make the decision quickly, and get out of her life, out of her space.

He seemed to fill it too forcefully.

After taking a gulp of her coffee, she went through to the cramped room beyond the kitchen that Dad used as an office. She grabbed the pile of papers he had prepared. There were surveyors' maps of the property, marked with various details, sheets of figures on fodder yields and winter feed requirements and the inventory of farm machinery included in the sale.

Piling all of it in front of Lucas at the kitchen table where he sat, she said, "Here. Maybe you'd like to take a look at some of this while you drink your coffee. So we don't waste time."

She stressed the word "we" just a little. She could have been out with the hands today, refencing the stackyards or putting out salt. Instead, she had to spend her time with a man who planned to bulldoze her home and didn't mind telling her so.

Except that when she'd tried to attack back, she almost thought she'd seen a spark of something softer in him. Understanding. Or even a wistful kind of envy. It sparked an unwilling curiosity inside her, which smoldered slowly, the way a carelessly thrown cigarette butt smoldered in dry summer heat before setting a whole forest on fire.

He took a mouthful of coffee, which left a film of the thin black liquid glistening on his lower lip. Then he sat back in his chair and twisted a little, to take in the view. He hadn't looked at the papers she'd given him.

"This is great," he said. His big shoulder pushed to within a few inches of her hip. From this angle she could see the way his dark lashes silhouetted against his cheeks.

"I hope you mean the coffee." She took a step back, out of his space.

"Actually I meant the whole—" He stopped.

She glared at him, silently daring him to mention bulldozers again.

You want to praise the vista from the windows of a house you're planning to tear down, Mr. Halliday? I don't think so!

"Yes, I mean the coffee," he agreed. "Great coffee."

His mouth closed firmly over the last word.

No smile.

He lifted his mug toward his lips, met her spark spitting eyes with his, and if there was any kind of apology there, any kind of understanding, or the vulnerability she thought she'd seen before, he didn't let it show. His gaze held hers, narrow-eyed and thoughtful. Arm and mug froze midair.

She felt herself getting hot.

Aware.

She hadn't ever responded physically to a man this fast, and didn't know why it was happening. She'd met impressive looking men before. Was it the adrenaline of wanting to fight this one, over the ranch?

Gee, that made sense—to link attraction and fight.

"Look," he said, "I know you probably would have preferred for Jim to give me this tour."

"Might have helped." She folded her arms across her chest and hunched her shoulders, resisting the pull she didn't want. "I've lived here my whole life. I'm not looking forward to this."

"It's the selling and leaving, surely, not the thought of the changes a buyer will make." His eyes were steady and clear. "Any buyer is going to make changes."

"I'd prefer not to hear about them, if I don't have to."

"You're going to stay in the area, right?"

"I plan to, yes, at this stage." In fact, she still felt very uncertain about what she wanted from her future. She loved it here so much.

He shrugged, as if nothing more needed saying.

Okay, so he had a point. Burying her head in the sand would be impractical and impossible, if she stayed in Biggins. A buyer could make worse changes than bulldozing a very ordinary home that just happened to have been hers for twenty-six years, and her family's for a lot longer.

She set her mouth tight, detesting Lucas Halliday for being right, for being up front about it like this, for making her nerve endings sing without even knowing it and for apparently understanding that bluntness was just a little easier on her spirit than empathy would have been.

"I'm sorry this task is falling to you," he said. Each word

came out measured and matter-of-fact. "But my father will expect the kind of detail I can only get from someone who really knows the place. If it's any consolation, he's not going to haggle over the price if I tell him this is the ranch he wants, and he's keen to push the purchase through quickly."

He spread his hands in a gesture that almost looked like an apology. "Raine, my stepmother, wants a white Christmas in a log cabin this year."

"We can do the log cabin," she answered, just as matter-of-fact. "No guarantees on the snow. There, you'll have to negotiate with a higher power. Got any favors you can call in?"

He laughed. It should have eased the atmosphere, but it didn't. Drinking her coffee in clumsy gulps, Reba watched him page through the documents and papers she'd laid out. He drank absently, giving the impression that he hardly tasted the strong brew, and he thudded the mug down on the table top between mouthfuls.

He took out a pocket calculator and keyed in several sets of figures, absorbed in his assessment. Was he checking Dad's math? He scribbled some lines in a pocket-size notebook.

Uncomfortable about watching him, Reba retreated behind the breakfast bar. She wiped down the stove top, cleaned the crumb tray beneath the toaster and watered the row of African violets on the windowsill above the sink.

She almost watered Lucas Halliday himself, while she was at it. He'd come to the sink to return his mug. She'd been filling the little tin watering can again and hadn't heard him, his movements masked by the sound of water drumming on metal. When she turned with the filled can, intending to water the flowering cyclamens in her parents' room, as well, they came face to face and can to chest.

"Whoa!" He grabbed the pouring end of the can and a spray of drops darkened across the arm of his sweater.

"Oops."

"No problem."

He still had the mug. She snatched it from him too abruptly, turned and put it and the watering can on the draining board.

She could feel him still standing right behind her, feel him through to her bones, to the roots of her hair and to the walls of her lungs, which suddenly refused to draw breath. The strength of his pull on her body shocked her, and she heard his next words with a rush of relief.

"Ready to head outside?"

Reba kept both of them busy the whole morning. She did the job delegated to her by Jim Broadbent and her father, and she did it well, Lucas considered. It was painfully apparent how much she cared about this place, although she struggled hard not to show it. Again, with a hot pool of envy low in his gut, he wondered how that would feel.

Not useful, in a situation like this, when the family had to sell.

He should be grateful he'd never have the same problem.

They looked over almost every piece of infrastructure and equipment included in the sale. Calving barn, corrals, machinery sheds, scale room, tack room and bunkhouse. Pickups, stock trailers, haying equipment, round baler, swather and bale feed. A semi-Kenworth tractor, a tractor with loader... The list went on and on, and didn't deviate from the list both Reba and Jim Broadbent had already given him.

Everything seemed well-maintained, and when it wasn't, Reba said so. "This flatbed needs new tires," and "One of the four-wheelers isn't running right."

Lucas lost count of how many times he saw her denim-clad hip hike up at an angle, and her neatly rounded backside slide across the torn seat of the battered ranch pickup as she climbed in to the driver's seat. He got to know the sound of the gears and the clutch, like a strand of familiar music, and the smell of dust and grass and engine oil like a neighbor's brand of tobacco.

He'd never realized you could drive a pickup with such a high caloric expenditure. Reba didn't raise her voice and she never swore, but she wrenched the wheel around, lunged at the gearstick and floored accelerator and brake pedal as if driving was a form of hand-to-hand combat.

Every time they stopped, she slapped her pretty, callused hands on her thighs, yanked on the hand brake, looked at him with her big, bluey-greeny-grayish eyes—incredible eyes, because, seriously, what color could you possibly call them?—and announced, without smiling, "Scale shed," or "Lower Creek Field," as if they'd just navigated the Amazon River, and she navigated it every day.

"Is this pickup on my vehicle list?" he finally asked.

She drove it the same way she walked—not gracefully, but with a way of moving that kept grabbing his gaze and that, for some unknown reason, he liked. He'd handled a lot of vehicles in his time, but he wasn't sure that he'd be able to handle this one. Not without practice, anyhow.

The woman who sat beside him would take practice to handle, also. He found himself imagining a little too clearly what the rewards might be.

"You wouldn't want this one," she told him. "It's on its third time round the mileage clock, and it's got more temperament than a jumpy horse. Second gear pops out with no warning. It stalls under a thousand revs, and it drinks oil like I drink coffee. Can't get through the day without a big top-up, first thing every morning."

At the hay stacking yard in the Lower Creek Field, a couple of the hands were fixing fence, with a herd of mama cows looking on.

"They're bred," she told him. "They'll start calving in mid-March."

She introduced him to the ranch hands, Pete and Lon. The four of them ate a lunch of sandwiches, cookies and more coffee, standing up. The sun shone out of the pristine blue. Lucas's back felt hot, and his eyes tired from squinting.

He looked at one of the hands. Lon, he was pretty sure, but he might have gotten them mixed up. The man was standing bare-chested with his T-shirt tucked into the back of his jeans like a cleaning rag, and Lucas wished he could peel off his sweater. Inappropriate for the potential buyer of a high-priced ranch to be seen shirtless, unfortunately.

Reba looked hot, too.

When she thought no one was watching, she rolled her sleeves as far as her smooth, soft biceps, and unfastened another button at the front of her shirt. She rewound the red elastic around her ponytail, pulling it higher so that the thick, glossy hair swung free of her sweat-misted neck.

She had sunglasses on, but she mostly kept them pushed up on her head, as if she could see the detail of her beloved ranch more clearly without them. Lucas would have liked to borrow them, and wished he'd worn some of his own, to shield his city eyes against the bright light.

After they left Pete and Lon, she showed him the Upper Creek Field and they walked two hundred yards or more, along the bank of the fishing stream, with Lucas dropping behind her, letting her lead the way.

I'm not doing this so I can watch her walk, am I? he thought, a little disturbed at the idea when he realized he was. That purposeful, rolling stride, that tight, shapely denim butt.

Too distracting.

Too enticing.

Not on the agenda.

He kicked along faster and caught up to her in four strides, in time to hear her telling him, "A little farther on, we'll be able to glimpse the gaming cabin."

Then she spotted an untidy shape in the grass and they both realized it was a cow, long dead, that had somehow escaped the vigilance of the ranch hands. She frowned at the sight, gave a hiss of breath and narrowed her incredible eyes, with their dark fringed lashes.

Lucas reached out and touched her shoulder, expecting that she'd turn into his arms for a moment's support, wanting her to do it. He felt soft flannel over warm bone, and let his hand slide down to her bare arm, which was even warmer and softer.

A rush of intense desire powered through his body and snatched the air from his lungs. He could have sworn she felt it, too. He heard the awareness as a new rhythm in her breathing, and felt the midday heat of their bodies mingle.

After just a moment, however, she flicked off the contact like a horse flicking a fly, then hugged her arms around herself and pivoted away. "Too late to do anything about it, now."

"I'm afraid so," he answered.

"I'll tell Lon about it when we get back." She let a beat of silence hang in the air, then said, "Look, can you see the movement in the stream?"

Lucas knew something about trout, Reba soon realized,

so she didn't need to point out which were browns or cut-throats or rainbows. The plentiful fish gleamed beneath the water like painted foil. The current braided transparent patterns on the streambed and babbled nonsense songs in the clear air.

The walk took twenty minutes, because they did it slowly. Neither of them talked very much at all. The sun shone. The wind riffled the trees. Reba liked the silence, and she liked that Lucas Halliday knew how to be silent. Some people didn't.

"Here's the place where we can see the cabin," she told him, stopping beside a still, shaded pool.

She'd been aiming for this spot. From here, they should turn back.

"Yeah? Can you show me?"

He seemed interested, but she still didn't know what he was thinking, or what mental notes he'd made for the report he'd present to his father. No point in wondering about it, she told herself again. His intention would become apparent with time.

"Well," she said, "there's a ridge line coming down to the water about two hundred yards upstream, can you see it?"

Standing beside her, only a little behind, Lucas followed the arrow of Reba's arm. "With a seam of rock showing below the trees?"

"That's it," she said. "Follow it up. There's a downed tree, a ponderosa pine, making a kind of notch about two thirds of the way to the top."

"This time, I'm not seeing it." He leaned closer, cursing hours of computer screens two feet from his face, trying to use her arm like a rifle sight.

He caught the waft of her scent and it hit him like heat haze rising from a tarred road. Sunscreen predominated, with afternotes of hot, clean hair and sun-dried cotton. Why should things like that smell so good? He was more accustomed to designer perfume, but his body told him that this was better.

Way better.

"Look for a slash of paler color. A lightning bolt opened up the trunk like matchwood this summer."

"Okay, got it," he answered. His shoulder brushed against her back, and he felt a flicker of movement from her. Vibration, rather than movement. She didn't ease away, and her voice rose in pitch, dropped in volume and filled with breath.

No doubt. She felt it, too.

"Directly behind it, you can see the roof of the cabin, in the fold of the next slope," she said.

"Yes. Dark shingles, and the line of a window frame?" He could feel the swell and fall of her breathing, and he could still smell her hot, cottony, beachy fragrance.

"That's it," she told him. "It's beautiful up there, but we hardly use the place anymore. My grandfather used to bring hunting parties up there all the time."

"Show me tomorrow?"

"Do you ride?"

"Some. When I can."

"Then we'll ride up. After the trip to Steamboat Springs in the morning."

"Sounds great." He turned his face ninety degrees in her direction and grinned at her.

He was just inches away from her, now, and was sorely tempted to move even closer, to see what she'd do, to test this powerful pull. Her eyes were like mist over ocean, or rain on a summer pond. His shoulder slid across her spine with slow, deliberate pressure, and he stepped back, before she could fight him.

No, before she could lean into him. Yes, that's what she would have done, he realized. She would have leaned against him. She knew it, and though a part of her wasn't happy about that, the rest of her didn't care.

He didn't push the moment, or push her reaction. He didn't particularly want to get slapped in the face right now, and a slap in the face was a definite possibility. Nor did he want to add any more of an emotional element to a potential business transaction that had already become too personal for his taste.

He wasn't used to this.

"I think I've seen enough for today," he told her, and he meant Reba herself as much as he meant her ranch.

Chapter Three

"Tell me what you regret about last November," Lucas said to Reba. "What should I have done differently? What would *you* have done differently? Tell me what you resent in how I handled everything from the very beginning, September included."

His eyes flicked to Reba's pregnant stomach and he frowned. They hadn't gotten to the nitty gritty, yet. They were both still caught up in memories about their first meeting that were still achingly vivid, even after almost six months.

Reba searched for the right answer to his question, while the nagging, belt-tightening ache in her back and stomach notched a little higher on the pain scale, slower to let go, this time. She didn't like it. It made her uneasy. She reached for the inadequate chair at the manager's desk and eased herself into it, making it squeak, just as the door opened, hard on the sound of a token knock.

"Gordie's here, looking for you," one of the waitresses said.

Churned up and uneasy, she couldn't school the impatience out of her voice. "Oh, *now?*"

"What shall I tell him?"

"Tell him I'm— Tell him—"

"Tell him to wake up to the fact that he's not wanted, and hasn't been for eight months or more," Lucas answered for her, then revised at once, "No, just tell him she's not here. Let him work out the rest for himself." The waitress nodded, the door closed, and he added to Reba, "McConnell's still around. Is he back in the picture, then?"

"No, he's not."

Reba felt quite positive on this subject.

Gordie himself vacillated like waterweed in a river current, however. His attitude back in September had pushed her right into Lucas's arms, she sometimes felt. He'd hung around the steakhouse, the way he still hung around. He'd given with one hand and taken away with the other, and he was still doing it.

After showing Lucas around the ranch that first day, she'd worked a shift at the steakhouse the same night, venting her complicated feelings about the sale and the man by throwing her steaks roughly around the grill. It hadn't helped. She was still feeling tense and angry and confused when Gordie had sloped into the kitchen to hang out with her, and maybe that was the real point where it had all started with Lucas…

"Hi, Reb." Gordie had dragged a stool in from the bar and positioned himself on it in front of the big freezer. He already had a light beer in his hand.

"Hi, yourself," Reba had answered. Her smile was an effort. "No food in your fridge, tonight?"

She tried to make it into a tease, but found it irritating that he still came in here like this, so often. And she was tired, after too much tension with Lucas Halliday today, while she'd showed him over the ranch, so she had to fight to hide the irritation.

She and Gordie had broken up two months ago, for heaven's sake! Maybe she should be pleased that they could still be friends, as far as he was concerned. True, she did feel a certain degree of relief. She wouldn't want to think that she'd hurt him so badly he couldn't stand her company. In a small ranching town like Biggins, when she cooked four shifts a week at the only decent restaurant, that would be awkward for a whole lot of people.

But it made her uncomfortable that his routine had been so little changed by her calling off their engagement. He should have started serial dating around three counties, or something. He should have brought strange blondes in here to dangle in front of her, every week. He should at least have had his hair cut different, and bought a couple of new shirts.

Like I've done any of that? she scolded herself, as she watched him take a gulp of his beer.

"I've been thinking, Reb," he said, ruffling his choppy dark hair at the back with his spare hand. It stuck up after he'd finished with it, definitely getting too long.

He was the only person who called her Reb. She didn't mind it from him. She didn't challenge the statement that he'd been thinking, either. He had a good brain, especially for figures. She didn't possess one herself. He had statistics on his computer, relating to the McConnell ranch, that even her father wouldn't have thought to tabulate. He spent a lot of time on the Internet, which apparently made money for him, she wasn't even sure how. And he could ride as if his thighs were part of the horse.

"Yeah?" she answered, slinging three steaks on the grill.

"You've got a buyer sniffing around, right?"

"He seems interested. But he's a businessman. Pretty hardheaded." Enough to bulldoze my family home. "He's not going to make a spur-of-the-moment decision. He wants to see more tomorrow, so I'm taking him down to Steamboat, and up to the cabin."

"Because I've been thinking."

"You said that." She smiled, to soften the statement, and wished once again that he wasn't here. Or that he was somehow different. Tougher? With more emotional perception in his heart?

"If we got married after all, your Dad might decide not to sell," he said. "I'd be willing."

At this, she had to fight to stop her jaw dropping open. "We broke it off, Gordie," she reminded him, then added more bluntly, "*I* broke it off."

"Yeah, I know, but nothing much has changed since then, has it? For either of us? Except that your Dad is selling the ranch."

"There's that, yes," she answered heavily.

"So I wondered… I kind of was relieved when you broke it off, but now I'm thinking we were both too hasty. We had a good thing going, and I should have talked you out of it, instead of feeling—"

"Gordon McConnell…!"

"Not to insult you, or anything."

"Because you were *kind of* relieved?" She plated two ribeyes, and threw a glance over the grill to see if anything else needed flipping.

"I just— You make me nervous, Reb."

"What do you mean by that?" Her anger rose inside her.

"You scare me. The way you're so— But that's okay. If you could just—"

"Let's get this straight, here! Are you asking me to *change,* so that you could stand to marry me, so that we could keep Seven Mile in the family?"

He blinked his light blue eyes. "Just tone down a bit. Don't feel stuff so much. Don't get so emotional and passionate about everything. Is all. Makes me nervous. See, you're doing it now!"

Damn right she was!

Damn right she was emotional!

And apparently it showed. The clenched teeth and the half growl, half shriek that escaped from between the clenched teeth gave a clue.

"I don't think we should get married, Gordie," she said. With difficulty, she kept the lid on the passion that he regretfully, tactfully, didn't want as part of the Rebecca Grant package.

He flinched a little, then argued, "But you want to keep the ranch."

He'd always been persistent.

"No, I don't," she yelled, over the hiss of cooking steak. "I spent all day today, showing that buyer over the place, and he's ideal. Rich. Smart. Experienced."

Interesting. Complex. Hot.

"If he's serious, I couldn't be happier," she went on. "Mom and Dad deserve to have the best lifestyle they can, down in Florida. I'm glad I scare you, Gordie, because you're beginning to scare me!"

"So now you know how it feels. Just tone down. I care about you. You know that. We're good together."

They were terrible together!

They'd been terrible together for more years than she cared to count, and they'd always had more habit than passion in the mix. She hadn't questioned this because he rode so well and he ranched so well. He had the organizational skills, number skills and money skills that she lacked. On paper, he was perfect for her, and his ranch was right across the fence.

And she'd been holding her breath about Mom's health for so long, she hadn't wanted to rock any boats. Wanting to stay safe, she'd hidden her head in the sand, but safety had proved an illusion.

She couldn't even remember the immediate trigger that had prompted her to tell him it was over. Thinking back, she decided there wasn't one.

They hadn't had a fight. She hadn't met someone else. She'd just reached some invisible line in the sand and cracked.

Exploded.

And the fallout and shrapnel was still in the air. She'd realized that this wasn't her life. Watching Gordie Mc-Connell sit on a bar stool drinking beer while she cooked, telling her to "tone down" just wasn't her life.

He'd said the toning down thing to her before, she remembered, but she'd never understood what he meant, never paid it the right attention. And it might be someone else's life, but it wasn't hers.

So what's mine?

She didn't know.

Meanwhile, Gordie hung out in the kitchen for another half hour, while in her mind Reba watched the pieces of her exploded self still hanging in the air. She had no idea where they would eventually fall, and she didn't trust this odd new intuition that Lucas Halliday could somehow help her find out.

She felt a sudden need to explore the intuition, all the same.

* * *

As arranged, Lucas arrived at Seven Mile early the next morning in his rental car.

Reba had told him she'd show him the shortcut from the ranch down to Steamboat Springs. On the way back, they would make a couple of detours. He wanted to look at trout streams and hunt down the elusive herd of wild horses that roamed the Medicine Bow Range. The round trip would probably take a good six hours, apparently, plus a stop for lunch, so she'd suggested they start at seven.

She seemed different, this morning, he thought.

The same electric current ran through her veins that he'd seen in her all of yesterday, but today it was… Bolder? More open? Less angry, but even more determined. She was proving something to somebody, with those sparking eyes and that jutting jaw. Lucas didn't know what it was, or who she was proving it to, and maybe she didn't, either, but it was a pretty impressive sight.

Today, he drove while she navigated. He thought they might clash over the new roles, but they didn't. She told him where to turn in plenty of time, which let him relax and focus on the drive.

And on her.

The Indian summer temperature was forecast to flare even higher today. She wore shorts in anticipation, although at this hour a dawn chill still lay on the land. The honey-beige of the shorts matched the tan on her legs and drew his attention to how long and smooth they were, stretching down to a newer, shinier version of yesterday's boots.

A baggy, dark navy sweatshirt hid the rest of her. Its round neckline half covered a thin gold chain she hadn't been wearing yesterday, and showed the occasional glimpse of something white—a tank-top shoulder strap, or possibly her bra.

She had her hair looped and knotted at the back, with some sexy little tendrils already escaping. She even wore makeup. It made her eyes more startling than ever in their unusual color. Her lips were darker and redder, and he noticed them every time she spoke, every time he dared take his eyes from the road to look sideways.

Yesterday, she'd dressed down for him. Today, she'd apparently dressed up, in her own way, for wild horses and Steamboat Springs.

Heck, how long was it since he'd met a woman who considered polished riding boots a big step up on the fashion ladder?

For most of the drive, he forgot to think about what Dad or Raine would want if they were here. Raine hated hair-raising roads with no guardrails and steep drops. She hated getting dust on the car. Actually the car rental company might not be too thrilled about that, either.

Hair-raising roads with no guard rails and steep drops didn't seem to trouble Reba Grant. The temperature climbed and she took off her sweatshirt. Yes, the white fabric did belong to a tank-top—a little stretchy cotton thing with a triangular panel of lace in front. It fit snugly over her curves and her ribs, and he could faintly see the pretty shape of a white bra beneath it.

Using the discarded sweatshirt for a pillow behind her head, she slid her seat back and stretched her long legs out in front. She pointed out wildlife and vistas and potholes in the road with a combination of familiarity and fresh interest that sparked his own curiosity.

"You sat up like a startled cat just now, but you must have seen elk around here before."

"Sometimes you forget to look, when you've seen something before. You take it for granted. I told myself I wasn't going to do that today."

"Because you're selling? Because you won't be here any more? I thought you were staying in Biggins."

"I want to. Wanted to," Reba corrected herself.

Yesterday, she would have resented Lucas probing her on personal issues like this. Today, she wanted to talk, and still had last night's odd sense that he could be the right person to listen.

Something about his eyes.

The perception.

The blunt honesty.

He'd talked about bulldozing her home. Bluntness could be refreshing, sometimes. It could be *necessary.* Even if she got angry with him, anger could give clarity, the way it had last night, with Gordie. She couldn't simply wait for the explosion in her life to settle. She had to go out and look for the pieces.

"I didn't really consider the alternatives," she went on. "I don't want to move to Florida. I'm not sure what there would be for me there. I love this country." She took a breath of the mint-clean morning air flooding through the half-open window. "But I don't want to end up twenty years from now, still a short-order cook at the same restaurant, with corns on my feet and dreams that faded before I even knew I had them—"

"Can't picture you like that, for sure."

"—because I never had the courage or took the time to really think about the future. This is a—a huge turning point. I don't want to just let it happen to me."

His glance arrowed across in her direction. As usual he seemed to take her whole soul in at a glance. And her whole body. "You don't want your father to sell the ranch. That's clear. Jim Broadbent said your mother's health made the decision. She has lupus, right?"

"Systemic Lupus Erythematosis, yes."

She hated the disease, hated its long, unpronounceable name. Some people called it SLE, which was snappy, at least. It had variable, wandering symptoms that were unique to each person. It had unpredictable phases of exacerbation and remission, and it could kill Mom eventually, if her kidneys failed or the disease reached other vital organs. Those worst case scenarios might not occur for years, or ever, but she'd never be cured.

"And your dad wouldn't consider leaving the place for you to run?"

"No, they need the money. But I couldn't run it. My brain's not built that way."

"You seem pretty bright to me, and totally at home around the ranch."

"It's not just about doing the right chores at the right time. It's a business. You'd know that. I don't have a business brain. I'd have to get a really competent manager, which would eat up too much cash flow, on top of the wages for the hands and everything else."

"It could still be a profitable enterprise."

"All my parents' assets are tied up in Seven Mile Creek, and if they don't sell, they'll have to rent in Florida, and watch their pennies. Mom's medical bills are getting higher every year. No, the ranch has to be sold."

"But you'd prefer a local buyer, not me," Lucas said, pushing Reba a little. He wanted all of this clear, and out in the open. He wanted to understand the sources of this woman's anger, her unhappiness, and her fight.

Her voice dropped and slowed and took on a throaty

quality he knew she couldn't control, and maybe didn't even hear. She ran her palm down her bare thigh and he heard the light friction of her work-roughened skin. Palms like cardboard, legs like silk, inner thighs like whipped cream melting over apple—

Hell, he had to stop thinking about her this way... didn't he?

Did he?

Maybe she wanted him to.

Her eyes glared at him a lot, but the rest of her body said something different. Powerfully. His groin tightened and filled even more, and he stared ahead at the road, not daring to look sideways, in case he gave too much away. Or in case he caught fire.

She tilted her head, smiled a little, like a slow dawn breaking. "Actually, I'm getting used to you," she said.

All the way through brunch at Steamboat, a look around the resort, and a failed attempt to find the wild horses, all through the winding drive back, Reba felt the exhilarating prick of danger in Lucas Halliday's company.

Just yesterday, her emotional compass had been arrowed toward a hopeless need to protect the ranch, to protect the childhood she'd loved by staving off this big city buyer until a better one came along—a buyer like Gordie McConnell would have been, if he'd had the money, or the right claim on her heart.

She had wanted a buyer who would come into the steakhouse every night, regular as clockwork, tell her how the place was going and listen to everything she said about keeping it the same.

Today, everything was different.

Gordie was the only lover she'd ever had. He'd been in

her life too long, and had stopped her from seeing her future clearly. That was her fault as much as his, and she had to do something about it. Lucas Halliday seemed like part of the answer. She knew he wouldn't be looking for anything beyond a short-lived flirtation. Why not respond, just a little, just to see how it felt?

It needn't go very far.

And yet if it did…

She'd never felt this way about a near-stranger before— this awareness that he wanted her and she wanted him, on a raw, physical level, immune to any other considerations. It made her dizzy, hungry, exultant, scared. The right kind of scared. Full of adrenaline and courage. She found that she liked it.

Back at the ranch after their long morning of touring in the car, he was ready to get on horseback right away, so she changed into jeans and her scuffed riding boots and took him out to the stable. She gave him her own mare, Ruby, while she took her father's gelding, Moe. Lucas hadn't big-noted his riding skills, but he found his way around the tack room without asking dumb questions, and mounted the sixteen-hand animal with ease. He'd be all right.

Reba loved this ride up to the cabin, and they couldn't have picked a better day for it. The fields shimmered in the heat and the air was scratchy with dust. However, once the horses had splashed through a shallow section of the stream to reach the forested mountain slopes beyond, the shade beneath the ponderosas struck cool on her hot body.

Neither she nor Lucas spoke very much as they rode. Saddles creaked, insects buzzed, horse shoes clapped like scattered applause on earth and grass and rock. Knowing the route, Reba led the way. She only turned back once in a while, to warn Lucas about a tricky section or point out something of interest.

It must have been around three in the afternoon, or a little later, when they reached the cabin, but she hadn't worn a watch, so she didn't know for sure. Dismounting, she looped Moe's reins around an old-fashioned hitching post, and Lucas did the same. She swung her day pack clear of her shoulders and brought out some carrots and apples as treats for the horses. They began to crunch on the offerings loudly.

Pretending to be absorbed in feeding them, and chewing on one of the two apples she'd saved, she watched Lucas covertly. He shaded his amber eyes with his hand and looked back the way they'd come. He had a folded crease in one leg of his bone-colored pants, after their ride, echoing the softer, darker crease he'd have in his skin, at just about the same point, where his thigh met his backside.

His back had to be hot under his black T-shirt, and he should be wearing a hat. The tan on that curve of neck would turn red, soon. Reba had sunblock in her day pack. She could offer him some. He would stretch his jaw and smooth the white liquid around that long, brown column, before handing the fragrant plastic bottle back to her. She could watch every movement.

She didn't make the offer.

What had captured his interest, down below, anyhow? You couldn't see the house or the outbuildings from here, but you could see the Bailey field and the Upper Creek field and a section of the road leading into Biggins. Felt as if they had to be a good two miles or more from the nearest human being.

Her heart shifted and sank. Maybe that was his exact thought. He'd probably consider it way too isolated, up here. His interest in the ranch, on his father's behalf, would turn out to be a frivolous city slicker impulse, and wouldn't survive this afternoon of reality.

"This place have electricity?" he asked, confirming her fear as he turned and came toward her again.

"Generator."

"And tanked roof runoff for water." He'd obviously seen the galvanized piping, and the tank that stood behind the cabin.

"It's not meant for year-round living." She heard defensiveness raising the pitch of her voice. "If you want your stepmother to have her white Christmas here, you'll need to haul some firewood. See, here's where the vehicle track comes out. We didn't take that, because it's longer, but you can get a pickup along it, or snowmobiles in winter. Easy."

He only nodded, walked over and stood at the head of the track, looking down it as far as the first bend. Turning again, he said, "Shall we take a look inside?"

"Sure."

Lucas let Reba go ahead of him, watching the tight way she held her body, the tight way she walked. He wanted to tell her it was okay, he wasn't going to get put off a major purchase because of one outdated hunting shack.

And even if he did decide against the place, on his father's behalf, Jim Broadbent was right. A buyer would show up soon. She could relax. Meanwhile, whatever happened with the sale, he had no intention of riding roughshod over her feelings.

He almost reached out to her with the same touch of support and understanding that she'd rejected yesterday when they'd spotted the dead beast, but she was too far in front, and the chance was lost.

For the moment.

But after the way she'd flirted with him in the car, his whole body was primed by the physical stretch of the recent ride and ached for its next opportunity.

The cabin wasn't locked, of course. The porch floorboards resonated beneath her feet, and by the time he'd stepped onto it behind her, she'd rattled the old door handle and swung the door open. He'd expected a dusty, musty interior, with dirt-misted window panes, uneven floors and shabby furnishings, but it wasn't like that at all.

"I came up here two days ago, cleaned it and aired it out," she explained. She'd even put fresh flowers in a couple of vases. There was the smell of lavender in the air. The furniture was old, true, but of good quality, and there were new throw pillows and slipcovers on the couch and two armchairs. The kitchen, also, must have been modernized only about ten years ago.

The old fireplace had been replaced with a modern, glass-fronted wood-burning stove. It was fan-forced, and would give out fantastic heat. You could slide the Persian-style rug closer, arrange the throw pillows in a heap on top, and sit here in front of it.

Toasting marshmallows.

Baking potatoes wrapped in foil.

Making love.

Hard to imagine, on an eighty-five-degree day, that such heat could be needed, but Lucas knew that temperatures could drop to thirty below, up here. Raine's white Christmas was a pretty safe bet.

The rooms were way too cramped for Raine's taste, though. He and Reba stood within touching distance because they had little choice. The windows were too small and the ceilings were too low. His stepmother would claim claustrophobia and boredom within a day.

Bulldoze the log cabin, too?

Absolutely not! Raine could build a new one, open plan, with twenty-foot ceilings, acres of glass and satellite TV, in some ostentatious location. Lucas would lay claim to this place for himself—his cut of the purchase, his finder's fee. It was an irrational, emotional impulse, and he wasn't sure why he felt it so strongly. He knew it didn't make sense. He knew it wasn't even his decision to make.

What was happening, here?

Too much.

More than flirtation.

Already, he understood more than he wanted to about why Reba's roots ran so deep into this soil.

"Do you want to see upstairs?" she asked him.

"Please." Sounded as if he were begging, and maybe he was.

She went ahead, denim rear end rocking as usual, and he followed closely, unable to tear himself free of her aura, so that when she suddenly turned and spoke, he was right behind. "I should have showed you the—"

The point she broke off was the point where his hand landed on her hip. Her body softened in an instant, and swayed toward him. Her eyes widened and went dark. Since he was one step below, her mouth was level with his, and only an inch away. He could feel her breath cooling his lip. She didn't attempt to increase the distance.

Good.

They'd gotten to this, at last.

He hadn't been sure that they would, and her huge eyes told him it might already be more than she'd expected.

He anchored her other hip in place, to keep the rest of her where she was, and watched her lips press together, then part again. She had another, more determined and even more doomed attempt at saying what she'd wanted to say before. "While we were downstairs, I should have showed you the—" Then she stopped again.

"Just show me the bedroom." His voice rasped, and the last word lost itself on her mouth.

Her lips were as warm and sweet as ripe fruit. They responded just the way he'd known they would. He closed his eyes. He didn't want to look, he only wanted to taste and feel. She stayed in place, thighs pressed to his groin, which meant she had to know just what her body had already done to him.

Oh, yes, she knew! She was overwhelmed by it, but she knew.

Did she know that she'd begun to shimmy against him, too? Her hips slid and rocked, slid and rocked. The movement went just an inch or two either way, and was oh-so-slow, but it made him throb and want to lunge. Her breasts, in their thin covering of lace and stretch cotton, jutted softly against his chest and he imagined her nipples, pebbled as hard as he was, from the slow friction between them.

How would they look, her nipples? Puckered with need? Definitely! Big and dark, or dainty and pink? He didn't care either way, he just wanted to know, see, touch and kiss.

"Show me the bed," he said.

Without waiting for her answer, he deepened the kiss, tangling his tongue in her mouth. He tasted the fresh, sweet apple she'd withheld from the horses several minutes ago. He abandoned her hips and slid his hands higher, trailed his fingertips across her breasts and thought, "Yes! I knew it. Like cherry stones."

She sank back with her spine arched. Suddenly she was seated on the wooden tread of the stairs, reaching up for him, eyes half-closed and hair threatening to tumble from its high knot. He went after her, chasing the taste of her mouth, chasing her body heat. He ended up bracing his fingers on the stair edge, his weight looming over her.

She pulled him lower. His face fell between her breasts and she gasped and threw her head to one side. He felt the heat-perfumed mass of her hair drift onto his hand. The soft mounds of her breasts against his cheeks and nose and lips felt like warm satin.

Her thighs parted and squeezed his ribs, half supporting him while he rolled a little. He slid her top up, clumsy with desire. Cupping her with one hand, he thumbed her hardened nipple, then replaced his thumb with his mouth, through a lace and net bra.

She dragged herself back, higher up the stairs, and held his face between her hands. Her eyes were still enormous, filled with a wild light and a soft flame of doubt. Throbbing, damming himself back, he realized she was still debating this. He pressed his lips together, struggling with a code of honor that said it had to be her own decision, made freely.

"Okay, I'll show you the bed," she said at last, on another gasp of air.

Her fingers feathered up his neck and into his hair and she stretched to kiss him, her mouth hungry and full of promise. Lucas discovered he was shaking, and that he hadn't breathed for the entire time she'd studied his face.

They scrambled the rest of the way up the stairs, breathless. There were just two bedrooms built into the roof line, both of them small, and he had to duck his head through the low doorway of the slightly larger one. Beside a double bed covered in fresh white sheets and a faded patchwork quilt, Reba crossed her arms, pulled her tank top over her head and unsnapped her bra.

Both garments fell to the floor in a pale heap and she turned to face him, straight-backed, arms at her sides, giving him the sight of her bare breasts and peaked nipples like a gift. Her eyes were huge and her breath came in shallow pants.

And he knew so totally that she *just—didn't—do—this,* she just didn't bring men to this cabin to make love, on a regular basis, or *ever.* Letting her make the decision on her own wasn't enough.

Not with a woman like Reba.

He knew what he wanted. Even if the corporation didn't buy the ranch, he wanted a piece of it to take away with him. He wanted a piece of Reba Grant, her passion and her intensity, to take away with him in the form of his memory of how she'd feel in his arms, writhing beneath his touch.

But knowing what he wanted wasn't good enough.

Instead of wrapping himself around her as he wanted to, instead of lifting her against him and pulling at her jeans, he allowed himself just one soft brush of his knuckles across those jutting gifts. They were fuller and rounder than he'd expected them to be, with the crests even bigger and darker than his imagination had painted them.

Then he placed his hands on the knobs of her shoulders, looked into her eyes and said, "Wait."

She seemed to understand exactly why he'd stopped. Instead of taking it as a way out, however, or even giving herself any further pause for thought, she lifted her chin, looked at him with narrowed, glittering eyes and said, "No."

"Why, Reba?"

"Because I want this. And so do you. Don't ask questions. Do me the courtesy of believing I know what I want."

"I'm not offering anything beyond—"

"I'm not asking for anything *beyond.* This is now. That's all. It's more than I—*way* more than I expected, even an hour ago, but—" she made her hand into a fist over her stomach "—it feels right, here. It feels necessary."

For another moment Lucas hesitated, and Reba felt the possibility of rejection slam into her.

Could he?

He couldn't!

He wanted this every bit as much as she did. She knew that. He hadn't denied it. The only way he'd reject her would be if some decent, chivalrous, protective instinct overcame him, and he decided that his making love to her right now was a favor she'd be better off without.

Despite the depth she'd glimpsed in him yesterday, Reba wasn't convinced that a corporate prince like Lucas Halliday possessed any such chivalrous instincts. She certainly didn't want him to possess them, right now. Gordie McConnell had them, and she was sick of them! Lucas was accurate in what he suspected about her narrow previous experience, and she didn't want that to get in the way.

Yes, Lucas, you're right, I've never done anything like this before.

Anything like this.

She and Gordie had made love, yes, but Gordie would never have done so in the middle of a working day, with no advance planning, in a location not previously designated as appropriate. And that *burned* her. So much about her life, and the crossroads she'd reached in it, burned her right now.

Dear Lord, she was nearly twenty-seven years old, she was about to have her home pulled out from under her like an old blanket off a horse's back. She was going to make love to Lucas now—a rough analysis of her mental calendar told her it should be safe—and she'd think about the ramifications later. She was going to do this before something in her soul atrophied into dry wood and she lost the ability to even imagine a different life for herself, let alone go out and find it!

"There's no doubt you know what you want." Lucas's voice caught on several of his words, and she felt his gaze on her peaked nipples like a caress. "Don't you care what I want?"

"If you don't want this…me…my body, then there's been something very wrong with your signals, since yesterday." She drew in a deep breath, felt her breasts lift, saw his tongue lap against his lower lip. His jeans strained at the front. He stepped closer to her, but not close enough.

"I'm talking about the ranch," he said.

"You think this is about—" Anger tightened her scalp. She dragged in a shaky breath and tried again. "You think I'm trying to sell you the ranch, right now, with this? That's— That's—"

"No! Hell, no, Reba!" Another step, urgent, that brought him toe to toe against her. He slid his hands up to her elbows. "I just wanted you to consider whether doing this— making love—" the word melted on his tongue like syrup "—would feel different if you knew my decision on the purchase."

Again, she didn't hesitate. "If you've made a decision, I don't want to know. Because it wouldn't make a difference. Okay?"

He nodded, touched her hair, her neck, let his hand trail lower, and bent his head to her mouth. "Yeah, you're right, I guess," he said, on a soft growl. "Wouldn't make a difference to me, either."

For the first time, she held him. She ran her palms up his strong back, and learned the pattern of his muscles, on either side of his spine. She helped him wrench the unwanted T-shirt up and over his head, put her tongue to her fingertip then, looking down, touched the moisture to his nipples. They hardened into little beads as it evaporated, and she felt a coil of pleasure and satisfaction deep inside.

She could do this to a man. She could do this to Lucas Halliday. And she wanted to do a whole lot more.

"Tell me what you like," she said, branding him with kisses between every phrase. "Show me. Touch me in all the places you want. With your hands. With your mouth. Teach me, Lucas."

"Hell, haven't you ever—?"

"Yes. Yes, I have. But not like this. Nothing like this." She reached for the front of his pants, fumbling a little as she snapped them open. She began to ease the zipper down, and he took a hissing breath. "Did I catch you?" she asked.

"No. Keep going. Yes, like that."

She did, even more slowly, feeling the straining ridge of cloth and man pushing at her hand. When he was free, she slid trousers and underwear down in one movement. She dropped low in front of him and let her mouth explore the texture of his thigh on the way. She knew exactly where he wanted to be touched, but kept that pleasure from him, stringing it out.

He couldn't stand it, pulled her back up and hauled her toward him so that they were pressed together from her breasts to her knees. His thigh eased between her legs, and she knew how hot she must feel to him, how full and ready.

"Take off your boots and your jeans," he said. "Let me look at you."

The old bed creaked as he sat and levered his own boots off. He kicked them beneath the bed, beyond the hem of the quilt, and she did the same. Then he watched while she shimmied her jeans down her hips, and she could tell he liked everything he saw.

"I didn't…uh…come equipped for this," he said, reaching for her. "If we need to set limits, can we set them now?"

"It's okay. The timing is— No limits." She brushed his mouth with hers, lifted his hands and brought them to her breasts.

"None?"

"Anything that feels good. Anything that's a part of this."

"Touching you, Reba, that's everything."

They kissed until her bones softened to liquid, and she no longer knew where her body ended and his began. His mouth was everywhere. She gripped him the way she'd have gripped a bolting horse, only who was bolting, who was out of control? Him, or her?

She leaned back on her hands and he knelt in front of her, on the braided woollen rug, trailing his lips down her jaw, her neck, to her breasts and beyond, to her sweet core. She bucked and twisted and sank into the bed, clenched her fists against the flood that swept her away, then felt him slide higher and seek entry. She was so swollen and ready that he slipped into her in a single movement, and a sound wrenched out of him, making his body vibrate against her chest.

"Reba, you're so beautiful, so strong. The way you moved just now…"

He thrust and she rocked, clinging to him, digging her fingers into the muscles of his back. She loved his weight on top of her and the almond smell of his hair in every breath she took.

Their climax came freely, and ebbed in a series of aftershocks that jerked both their bodies like whips. Reba didn't know what to say, whether to say anything at all, so she kissed him again, touching her mouth to his softly, as if each kiss was a word of tenderness or thanks.

"Hey…" he finally whispered.

"Hey," she answered back.

Chapter Four

"**Y**ou okay?" Lucas asked. He was watching the way
Reba winced and shifted in the unforgiving, creaky office
chair, his eyes bright with perception, as usual—perception and suspicion.

And, yes, okay, she didn't feel very comfortable right
now. Who could, with this tightness coming and going?
The pregnancy book she'd bought talked about false contractions—irregular, tight rather than painful, normal and
nothing to worry about. This was apparently them, and normal or not, she didn't like them.

There wasn't a lot of tenderness in Lucas's question, she
noted. The hard, calculating shell of a successful business
man appeared to be back in place, making Reba question
the other qualities she had thought she'd discovered in him
last September, as well as the heat and exhilaration and

happiness she would have sworn they'd both felt, the first time they'd made love.

"My back's a little sore, that's all," she answered him, playing it down. "I've been on my feet a bit too long tonight."

As soon as she'd waded through this confrontation with Lucas, she would ask Carla about the way her body felt and the way it should feel. She would consult the doctor, give in her notice to the steakhouse management tomorrow, spend the next three months flat out in bed, if she had to.

"You're looking after yourself, I hope," Lucas said. "You're getting the proper prenatal care?" Again, it sounded like an accusation, rather than a sign of his concern. Where was the man who'd lain in bed with her, so hungry and so tender?

Reba lifted her chin. "The doctor thinks I'm doing great, especially considering the one I lost."

"Is that what happened? Is that possible?"

"Yes!" Her scalp prickled with anger, and acid rushed up into her throat. She carried a child fathered by a stranger, it seemed. "I lost this baby's twin, although I didn't realize I was still pregnant for another month and a half. Good grief, Lucas, you couldn't possibly believe I staged it, could you? Staged *any* of it? How could I?"

He shook his head and closed his eyes, as if totally at a loss, and images of last year flashed through their minds, once again. September and November, Indian summer and winter's first chill. They'd known too many different emotions together, in too short a time…

Reba sat in the Indian summer shade on the bank of the creek and watched Lucas casting his line for trout. He stood in the water in thigh-high wading boots borrowed from her father, with his legs braced wide against the current. The muscles in his back rippled and tightened as he whipped his body back then forward to make the cast.

For half a second, the nylon filament caught the sun and made a scribble of light against a background of cool green shade, then the delicate fly silently hit the water and the line disappeared. Lucas's whole focus arrowed to the task of working the rod and the line.

Reba's breath caught and tightened in her chest as she watched him. It was like vertigo, and she was frightened of it—not sorry that he would be leaving tomorrow morning. She would need some space by then, and some time to think without the storm of sensual distraction that built inside her whenever she was with him.

This relationship wasn't meant to last.

They both knew that.

It's a turning point, that's all, she thought. A window thrown open in my mind.

Lucas had already caught three good-size fish, enough to cook and eat outdoors for lunch, over an open fire. In the expectation that he would fish as well as he seemed to do everything else, Reba had packed the pickup truck with the appropriate accompaniments, and soon they would drive the mountain track up to the cabin, where her grandfather had once made the ring of stones that the Grant family had been using as a picnic hearth on summer days for nearly fifty years.

And she had no doubt as to what she and Lucas would do up there after the meal was over.

For the last time?

They ate the fresh fish with bread and butter and salt and lemon, washed down with ice-cold mouthfuls of light beer, and then they didn't have to say a word, they just doused the fire, opened the door of the cabin and went upstairs.

In the small, tidy bedroom, Reba wondered if she'd ever be able to come to this place again without thinking of Lucas. Their awareness of each other, and their impatience, seemed to crowd the air and make it sing.

She knew she'd remember it every time she saw the dappled light dancing through the windows as a breeze moved the tree branches, every time she smelled the scent of lavender, because of the flowers she'd put here and the home-made sachets that scented the cotton sheets.

Pulling her top over her head, she felt Lucas's touch sear across her body. His hands curved around her ribs, brushed across her breasts, made her neck tingle. They tried to help each other undress, but just ended up laughing and kissing, fighting their uncooperative clothing.

"Are we in a hurry, here, or something?" he whispered.

"So slow down."

"Can't."

"Neither can I."

They only managed to do that when they got to the really important part—the part where they couldn't talk anymore, because their breathing was coming too fast and every sense was too overwhelmed. Then he held her and slid into her with a teasing control that had her pulling at him, crying out for more, until they both exploded, with pulses of light behind her closed lids like fireworks, or stars.

That night, she drove into Biggins, parked her pickup quietly in the far corner of the steakhouse parking lot and slipped across Main Street to Lucas's motel. He took her into Cheyenne for a long, slow meal and then brought her back again.

"I'll need to head out of here pretty early tomorrow to make my flight to New York," he told her, at the door of his room.

"I'm not expecting a goodbye breakfast."

"My father should make his decision on the ranch within a few days. I'm sorry I can't tell you anything yet."

"Will you stop apologizing about everything, Lucas? It's fine."

"Yeah?" His eyes narrowed and his expression turned thoughtful, searching.

"You don't owe me anything," she insisted. "Not an offer of purchase on the ranch. Not some kind of 'I'll call you' line, whether you mean it or not. I don't think there's been anything in what either of us has said to each other or how we've acted over the past few days that's made me expect this to go on. It was right for now, that's all. And I'm happy. If you are."

"Very happy. Hadn't expected...any of this."

"No. Same here. Little gift from life, at the right time."

"The perfect time."

They looked at each other. For a long time. His gorgeous eyes glinted at her in the darkness. The shape of his mouth made her ache. The woodsy male scent of him enveloped her like a cloak and her center of gravity dropped to somewhere low, low in her belly and stayed there as hot and heavy as one of her grandfather's river-worn hearthstones licked by flame.

"This is supposed to be goodbye," Lucas said. "But... uh...do you want to come in for a minute?"

"You think it's only going to take a minute?" she whispered, winding her arms around his neck.

He groaned and muttered something, stole a hungry kiss from her mouth, and they barely made it through the door.

Three weeks later, she began to suspect that she had to be pregnant.

A test confirmed it, and in the second week of November, now feeling horribly nauseous for much of the time, Reba heard through the town grapevine that Lucas was back at the ranch, staying in her old family home now that the sale was finalized.

Time to bite the bullet.

From the neat little house in Biggins which she'd been renting since the move, she called Seven Mile as soon as she could. The phone number hadn't changed, which churned her up a little. She spoke to Lon, who was currently acting as ranch manager on a trial basis. He told her that Lucas was out helping the other hands haul the firewood up to the cabin. He should be back within the hour, for lunch.

Grabbing coat and hat and gloves, she jumped into the brand-new pickup Dad had bought for her after the sale, and drove out along familiar roads that she hadn't seen in nearly a month. The ranch always looked so beautiful to her eyes at this time of year after the early falls of snow, with icicles bearded on the fence wires and the fields glistening white.

This morning the sun shone, making the trunks of the cottonwood trees near the river look silvery yellow. On the mountain slopes that faced south, some of the new snow had already melted from the dark rocks, making patterns of contrasting color. A herd of cattle in the Lower Creek Field gave color to the landscape, also. She could have climbed through the fence, run to them across the snow and greeted them like old friends.

When she pulled up in front of the house, tires squeaking on the compacted snow, Lucas had just gotten in. He had an opened can of soup in his hand, and his nose still looked red from the cold.

If he was happy about seeing her again, or if he'd have

preferred her a thousand miles away with their sizzling connection safely in the past, neither emotion showed. But then, she didn't give much away, either, as she shook the snow off her boots and entered the warmth and familiarity of the kitchen. She didn't want him to guess how nervous and churned up she felt.

She couldn't help looking around. Easier than looking at Lucas. She saw new furniture, fairly plain but not cheap, and evidence of Lon's businesslike bachelor existence—lots of newspapers and boots. Lon himself wasn't around right now, which helped.

"See?" Lucas said. "It's still standing. Want to inspect the place?"

"That's not why I'm here."

"No, I didn't think it was, but—" He stopped, looked at her, waited for a moment, then added, "Want some soup? Grilled cheese sandwich?"

Her mouth began to water in a flood, another pregnancy symptom. She sat heavily in a chair that someone had pulled out from the table earlier. She should have eaten before she came here, because an empty stomach plus the thought of food equalled nausea, in seconds.

She only nodded at Lucas's offer of food, because she needed to overcome the nausea before she could speak.

He could tell something was wrong. He shook the can-shaped blob of soup into an already overheated cooking pot and it began to hiss, but he didn't stir it. Instead he stood in front of the stove, denim-clad legs slightly apart, shirt sleeves rolled, eyes watchful.

She went hot, remembering how stunningly good his body had felt under her hands, and how good it had tasted, during the four wild days of their affair. She remembered how well they'd talked, too, and how much they'd laughed, safe within the limits they'd set on what was happening.

But then the nausea intervened again, and he became purely the near-stranger who'd fathered all these astonishing new feelings inside her.

"I'm pregnant, Lucas," she said.

A beat of silence filled the air, then, "Hu-u-h, what? *What?*" She could almost feel his scalp prickling and his heart rate speeding up.

"That first time up at the cabin, six weeks ago, before we used—"

"Okay." He whooshed out a long breath. "Okay."

He must have gone dizzy with reaction, or limp, or something, because he wheeled around and bent over the bench top, the soup can still in his hand, and leaned his weight on his forearms. The jagged can lid stuck up at an angle, attached to the rim at one point, and Reba had a ridiculous fear that he would cut himself. She almost went to extricate the can from his grip, but the nausea held her in place, and before she could move, he spoke again.

"You said it wasn't possible, that day. Didn't you?"

"I thought it wasn't. I guess I know too much about cow biology and not enough about my own." The humor didn't work.

"Have you decided what you're going to do?" He straightened slowly, and put the can down at last. The soup hissed and bubbled and threatened to burn.

"Is there any decision to make?" she said. "I'm having a baby, in around seven months. Our baby."

"So what have you decided to do?" he repeated. "Will you keep it?" His voice was careful.

So was hers, hiding a growing anger. "You don't want any input in this, obviously."

Silence. She could see his mind ticking over.

"You've had just a little more time to think about it than I have. Don't forget that, Reba," he said.

The words came out low and heartfelt and oddly gentle, and she knew she'd been wrong to react with anger. Her heart flipped suddenly. She never would have slept with him if she hadn't believed him to be a lot more than just a hardheaded business man, and she should remember that.

Cling to it, even.

Count on it?

"Don't jump to any conclusions, okay?" he added.

"I—I'll try."

She waited some more, her head buzzing and her body stiff and still queasy. "Do you consider that I have the right to any input?" he finally asked.

"It's not about rights, is it? It's about what you want, what you feel."

"No, I think it's about rights."

The word sounded arid, and it disappointed her, but she answered carefully, "Okay."

"The baby's rights. Yours. Mine. In that order, probably. The baby—" He broke off, gave a laugh that was almost a bark, as if the word baby was the punch line to some kind of twisted joke, then tried again. "The baby—sheesh!—will be shaped by whatever we decide. And you're the one who has to go through the physical part." He gave her a sharp, assessing glance. "Looks like you're going through some of it now."

She had her mouth hidden behind a fist, and only just managed to tell him, "Soup would help."

"Right." He turned to the stove, added the cup of water, at last, and began to stir.

The appetizing beefy smell reached her, and her mouth

filled again. She was grateful that he didn't try for any more conversation until he'd set a steaming bowl in front of her, along with a spoon and a packet of oyster crackers.

He put a hand on her shoulder, and gave a caress that was rough and tender at the same time.

"I only know one thing, right now," he said. "We're going to make something good out of this, for the baby's sake. We've created a life, out of one pretty amazing afternoon, and we're not going to wreck it. That's about rights, not feelings. We just don't have the right to wreck our baby's life."

Reba burst into tears.

Lucas opened the door to her the next morning with his ear pressed to his cordless phone.

"Hang on a second, John," he said into it, then to Reba, "Can I sit you in the kitchen, get you something to drink, or whatever and finish this call?"

"Just a glass of water, thanks."

She sat and sipped, trying to focus on the light November snowflakes falling outside. Lucas disappeared toward the bedroom end of the house to finish his call. Tension had brought her first trimester nausea to its height, however, and the water wasn't enough. Breakfast wouldn't stick around for much longer.

She dove for the bathroom.

Five minutes later, feeling a lot better, she found a clean towel in the linen closet and pressed it to her face, which felt cold and tight from the freezing tap water she'd splashed onto it. Breathing deep, careful breaths, she heard the creak of floorboards as Lucas paced back and forth in her parents old bedroom, still on the phone.

People couldn't keep still when they talked on a cordless telephone. Reba had noticed this before, and Lucas seemed to be a worse offender than most. His voice came and went as he did figure eights between the bed, the closet and the partially open doorway. He must have heard her fleeing to the bathroom, but maybe he didn't realize she was still here.

"Yeah, that makes sense," she heard him say, then a moment later, "You're right, John. I want to take action on this. I want to do it. All I can do is put forward the idea, and see what she says." He listened for a bit, pacing as before. "Thanks. I'll be in touch soon, obviously." Another pause to listen. "You've been great on this. Take care, now. Bye."

Reba didn't try to hide the fact that she'd been close enough to hear his decisive voice. Lucas came out of the bedroom and she waited for him, leaning a hand on the wall of the corridor.

"You okay?" he asked, stopping in front of her. They hadn't gotten this close to each other, yesterday. Not face to face, anyhow.

"Uh, yeah. Getting used to it." She sighed. "Getting tired of it."

"It's normal, right?"

"According to the book."

"You haven't seen the doctor yet?"

"I have an appointment."

"You need someone to take care of you. You can have me, if you want."

He reached out and brushed his forefinger gently down her nose. Clearly he wasn't sure that she'd react well to the contact. When she didn't turn her head away, he slipped a strand of hair behind her ear and touched her neck, looking deep into her eyes.

She'd forgotten what a liquid, golden amber his were, and how much they'd had the power to stir her. She felt a wash of powerful emotion that stunned her and made her want to cry.

"I can have you?" she echoed, wits turned to cotton wool, legs as substantial as a ghost's. "In what sense, are we talking about?"

"To take care of you. To make sure you have what you need, and that everything's okay. I want to marry you, Reba." Before she could answer, he added, "That is, I think it would be a good idea."

"Why?"

"Lots of reasons. The rights of the baby should probably go at the top of the list, and your security a close second. And I'm there in the mix, too. We'd need to recognize that we haven't known each other long enough to make any promises about commitment. We'd want to draw up an agreement that would spell it all out, allow for the realistic possibility of divorce."

"Hmm, that's romantic. If we're allowing for divorce, why get married in the first place?"

"Don't you think you might want that for your child someday?" he said. "The emotional security of knowing that his or her parents were once married, even if it didn't last? If we don't get married, how many questions are you prepared to answer about our relationship, when our son or daughter is old enough to ask?"

"A lot of women have babies on their own."

"A lot of those women might jump at the chance to secure their baby's future by getting married, if the chance was offered. Yesterday, I needed time to think before we talked. Today, that's what you need."

"I— Yes."

"Think about it, Reba. Take some time. Don't make a decision right away. Just know that I've considered the idea, and I really want to do this."

He touched her face again, and for a moment she thought he was going to kiss her, touch that gorgeous mouth to her lips. They couldn't get enough of each other, two months ago. She'd lost count of how often they'd made love over those days. Oh, she could call it to mind so clearly!

Now, everything was different. Biting winds and snow on the ground, instead of Indian summer and thick, warm air. She had a different house and a new car and a future so unplanned for that she could only take it one day at a time.

Without having kissed her, not even wanting to kiss her, apparently, or not deeming it wise, Lucas had just proposed that they should bite off a whole chunk of future together and swallow it whole.

"You're right," Reba said. "I need to think."

She felt as if he'd offered her back the ranch, but she couldn't afford to think that way. The ranch belonged to his father's corporation, not to him. There was probably a whole complicated tangle of legal stuff relating to the Halliday Corporation. She wasn't getting the ranch back, and neither was her unborn child.

Lucas had talked about rights, not emotions.

"I need to think," she said again, even less steadily.

"Look, can I come into town tonight and pick you up? We'll drive into Laramie, or even Cheyenne, find some place quiet to eat where half the county isn't going to stop by at our table to say hello. If you've made a decision by then, we can talk about the implications."

"If I haven't?"

"If you haven't, we can…just talk. We're having a baby together. We don't feel badly toward one another. We should be able to forge a connection that's going to work at least as far as doing the best we can for our child."

She nodded, and closed her eyes. "Dinner tonight? I'd like that. Okay."

"Are you? Okay, I mean. You look—"

This time, she didn't let him touch her, but stepped back. "You want me to cry again, right, like yesterday? I don't think I can deal with too much tenderness from you right now, Lucas, without launching a flood. It's nothing personal. It's hormones."

She got out of there with a small amount of dignity still intact, went home, freshened up and phoned Carla, to ask if she could cover for her at the steakhouse tonight. Carla knew about the pregnancy, and she knew the baby wasn't Gordie's. So far, she'd managed not to ask whose it was. Reba loved her to death for that alone, but planned to tell her the truth soon.

"Sure, I can cover for you," Carla said. "Everything okay?"

"Um, is it normal for there to be a little bleeding at this stage? I had some this morning. No pain, or anything."

Carla let a beat of silence go by before she replied. "It can be. It depends."

"On what?"

"On whether there's anything else happening."

"Nothing seems to be."

"Then it's probably fine. But you should get it checked out."

"Yeah?" *Tell me not to panic, Carla,* she thought. *No matter what happens with Lucas, I want this baby. I want it more with every day that passes.*

"Don't panic, hon."

"Okay, then, I won't. Mind reader!"

"Take it easy. Let me take your shifts for the rest of the week."

"That sounds like panicking, to me."

"It's playing safe."

Reba almost asked Carla about Lucas's marriage proposal, also.

If she accepted it, would that be playing safe? In the end, she said nothing on the subject to her friend, just finished up the call with her emotions and her stomach still tight and churning.

Across the restaurant table from Reba that night, Lucas felt uncomfortably detached, split.

He'd orchestrated this evening with the finesse he'd been trained in most of his life. He'd chosen Cheyenne's best restaurant, and ordered champagne, even though he'd correctly guessed that Reba wouldn't drink more than a few sips. He'd bought her flowers and a gold and diamond bracelet—one that could be easily matched to an engagement ring later, if she wanted one.

She hadn't given him her answer, yet, although he was pretty confident she'd say yes.

He wanted to marry her, in the same way he always wanted to finalize a new acquisition to the Halliday corporate portfolio—because it made economic sense, and because it put him in control.

His lawyer and good friend John had laid out the facts very clearly on the phone today. Lucas would be legally obligated to contribute to the child's support whether married to its mother or not. And, barring a deliberate decision to disinherit in favor of someone else, the baby would be his legal heir. Far better to have it bear the Halliday name, and the cocooning sense of family approval that marriage would bring.

Given these advantages accruing to her as-yet-unborn child, Reba would surely want the marriage for the same reasons. Her baby's financial security would belong to it by right, instead of potentially needing to be fought for, with proof of paternity.

Still, Lucas wasn't so crass or so unwise as to overlook the traditional trimmings, and he wondered what level of intimacy the package should include. Tender words, and promises?

Reba looked so beautiful tonight, in a dark red dress that skimmed breasts already noticeably fuller, from pregnancy, than the last time he'd touched them. Since the rest of her body had shed a few pounds, she no longer had the figure of a work-toughened rancher's daughter, but looked more like the artificially voluptuous, gym slimmed women he was accustomed to.

She still moved the same way she used to, however, still smelled the same, and smiled the same and had the same incredible eyes. He wanted her with an impatient intensity that was almost like pain. It gripped him, wouldn't let him go, and wasn't dampened one iota by the fact that she seemed oblivious to it.

Locked away in the discomfort of early pregnancy, she didn't hunger for him as she had back in September. What would happen if he leaned across the table and brushed his mouth across those soft lips? Would he ignite the flaming responsiveness in her that he remembered so well? Or would she turn away?

Keep some control, Lucas, he coached himself. Feelings aren't relevant. We're only talking about what's right for our child.

As he watched, she put down her fork and stared at her plate, still half-filled. She rose a little in her seat, then sat again, frowning.

"What's the matter, Reba?"

"I think I need the bathroom." She pushed her chair back so roughly that it skewed sideways and hit the wall. Her face crumpled, but he only glimpsed her expression for a fraction of a second before she turned her back. Racing blindly for the bathroom, she bent forward at an angle, with her forearm curved across her lower stomach.

Pregnant women were said to need the bathroom a lot, Lucas reminded himself, and when they needed it, they needed it at once. She'd be back in two minutes, with a look of relief on her face. He forced himself to stay seated, argued himself out of his sudden ill-ease, looked at his watch. He'd give her five minutes, and then if she wasn't back… Rationally he was sure she would be.

She wasn't.

After the sixth and seventh long, long minutes, he went up to the head waiter and said, "Look, I'm worried about my…uh…fiancée." The word felt strange in his mouth. "Can I check in the bathroom to see if she's okay?"

"Of course, sir."

He knocked. "Reba?"

"Lucas…" The moment he heard the way she said his name, he knew something was wrong. Barging in without even looking at the feminine mirror and fittings, he heard her voice again, from behind the closed cubicle door. "Lucas, is that you?"

"What's wrong?" His voice was hoarse.

"I'm losing the baby." Hers was shaky, squeaky, shrill and tight with tears.

"How do you know? How can you know that? What's

happening?" The flat of his hand landed on the door like a blow, and his heart began to thud.

She told him what was happening, and he felt sick. "Let's go to the hospital," he said. "They can do something. They can save it."

"I don't think so." The words wobbled all over the place. He wanted to break down the door. "When cows—"

"Reba, sweetheart." His throat hurt. He wanted to hold her in his arms and never let her go, but she had the door locked. "You're not a cow."

But she was right. The baby couldn't be saved.

Hands wet on the wheel, Lucas screamed into the ambulance bay at the hospital, and someone screamed at him to get out again. They had an emergency transfer, they had a major highway smash, they had an ambulance due, they had a retrieval team flying in from Denver. He parked illegally farther along the curb, and got Reba inside.

The whole emergency department was frantic, and though the staff seemed caring, it wasn't the kind of big New York teaching hospital that Lucas was used to. It made him nervous. They had to wait for an hour, during which Reba's pain and bleeding eased.

For most of the time, Lucas held her hand as she lay in a curtained cubicle, or stroked her hair, feeling ill and helpless. Neither spoke very much. Then, finally, a doctor came—young, distracted, but certain about what he found.

"The cervix is open. From the amount of blood you've told me about, and from the fact that you had cramping and pain, yes, I'm sorry, you've lost the pregnancy. It's very common, especially this early, and especially with first pregnancies. Around twenty percent, maybe even as high as a third."

He told them to wait a while, if they needed to, until

Reba felt ready to leave. A nurse brought her a cup of water to sip on, and tissues for her tears. Those would have come in handy an hour ago. The handkerchief Lucas had given her was sodden.

The emergency department seemed quieter now. He sat beside her, sensing she still didn't want to talk, not sure if she wanted to be touched. He ached to touch her. She finished the water, then gave him a rusty little smile, as if she hadn't used those muscles for a long time, and wanted to check that they still worked.

"I guess we don't need to get married now, after all," she said in an empty voice.

He nodded carefully, and tried to think about what he felt. Care, yes. An empathy for her that ripped him up inside. He felt sorrow, too, but then, as he delved a little deeper, God have mercy, he also found something else.

The baby hadn't been real to him yet, in the way it had been real to her. The baby's conception was a complication that neither of them would have chosen, if the choice had been theirs to make. Marriage was something he hadn't considered for a second, before the news of her pregnancy.

And now the pregnancy was gone, swept away.

"I guess we don't, do we?" he answered.

He felt the treacherous whisper of relief grow a little, and he knew that for a long, horrible moment she could see it there on his face. She turned away from him, her face crumpled with anger and pain.

Chapter Five

"How could you have thought that any of that was faked?" Reba almost yelled at Lucas, in the cluttered privacy of the steakhouse manager's office. "The trip to the hospital, the anger because you were so clearly relieved there was no more reason to get married, the grief…"

"What, no woman in history has ever faked a pregnancy, or the loss of one?"

She drew herself up higher in the chair, even though it didn't feel good. "*I* haven't. I wouldn't. What you see is what you get, Lucas. I'd have thought you'd at least know that about me, after the time we spent together."

"Except if that's true, I'm having a hard time getting my head around the fact that you're still pregnant, you've known you were still pregnant for, what, three months…?"

"I went to my doctor, just after Christmas, and he ordered the scan that showed one baby with a beating heart," she explained.

"…and you didn't tell me? You crossed the street and disappeared into a store when you saw me coming. You knew you were still pregnant, that day, didn't you? And you didn't want me to guess."

"After your reaction when I lost the baby, I didn't consider that you needed to know."

He ignored this for a moment, and asked, "When are you planning to give up work?"

"I haven't decided, yet. I'd like to save a little more money, first."

This goal evaporated into complete unimportance when the band around her stomach did its sneaky little squeeze again. *Please God, my baby can sleep in a box. This doesn't mean anything, does it? It's normal. It's not like November, when the bleeding came.*

Lucas exploded at her statement about money, and swore. "Why didn't you come to me? The moment you found out you had a second baby that had survived, you should have told me, the way you did in the beginning, that day you came out to the ranch. You should have called me, at least, in New York."

"I figured you'd had your chance," she told him now. "Dear Lord, Lucas, you were relieved!"

"No, it was more complicated than that."

She didn't listen. "Do you think for a second that I couldn't see it? Was I going to confront you in the main street of town six weeks later and say, 'Um, excuse me, I've just discovered I'm actually still pregnant after all, so can we go back to the original plan?' Do you think for a second I'd have considered your proposal in the first place if I'd known you'd only suggested the idea, on your lawyer's advice, because it would have protected your right to more control over how our baby was raised? I felt like an idiot for getting distracted by your camouflage of champagne and flowers and taking you seriously enough to try and work out how I felt."

"That's not the issue."

"It is! It's the only issue. You had your chance to be the right kind of father to this baby, and you blew it, Lucas. I felt—and I feel—no obligation at all to give you another shot at being involved."

"You're wrong," he insisted. His jaw was rigid and his eyes cool. "On two counts, you're wrong. First, you don't know how much I grieved about what we lost. When I came in here tonight, it was in part to tell you that. I ached, Reba, all through the winter. Second, there's a principle at stake here that goes beyond the rights and wrongs in how either of us reacted. I'm this baby's father and I deserved to be told."

"Okay, well in that case consider that I just did."

Reba stood up awkwardly, signalling that their confrontation was over. Lucas knew the full truth now. Yes, she'd had a miscarriage back in November, but she'd been carrying twins, and one of the babies had survived.

That was it, as far as she was concerned.

Game over.

She wasn't interested in his financial support, didn't know if she believed his claim about grief, and she wasn't hurt—couldn't afford to be hurt—by the changed emotions that vibrated between them, in such contrast to what they'd felt that first afternoon at the cabin.

She would arrange for some moderate level of access if he wanted it, but he'd have to take her to court if he wanted a fifty-fifty share, and she doubted he'd feel strongly enough to do that. Marriage was out of the question, and she felt naive for having taken his proposal at face value, back in November, even for a second.

The next move was up to him, and he had more than three months to consider what it should be, before the baby was due to be born.

Wait a minute.

Three months?

Her body had other ideas on this subject.

Wait a minute...

For a moment, she thought it was all her imagination, a flashback to that awful night in November, but no, it was real—this really was happening—this warmth that shouldn't be there, between her legs—and she saw the same panic reflected in Lucas's face that she'd seen that night, and that she knew was in her own face right now.

"What's happening?" he said. "I can tell something's not right, Reba, so don't try to pretend."

If his eyes hadn't been locked on her face, he would have seen, and if the noise from the restaurant hadn't been so loud, he would have heard.

"My—my waters must have broken. Just now, when I stood up."

Her legs were already completely soaked inside their jeans, and so were her socks and sneakers. She knew instantly that this wasn't good, she didn't need to refer the issue to Carla's greater expertise. And she knew now, too late, that those ebbing and flowing pains in her back and stomach, all evening, had indeed meant more than just too many hours spent on her feet in front of a hot grill.

She had a moment to wonder, also, if the stress she'd felt lately—tonight!—could be a contributing factor, as well as the drive to provide for her baby, which had led her to keep her long steakhouse hours.

In other words, if this was her fault.

All her fault.

Most of what she felt, however, was sheer terror. She'd already lost and grieved for her baby's twin. She couldn't lose this one, too.

"What does that mean?" Lucas said. "Hell, I know what it means…"

"We need to get to the hospital."

He grabbed the phone on the manager's desk without another word and barked his way through the emergency call like the corporate bulldog he was. At a moment like this, there was something intensely reassuring about his take-charge attitude, the only thing Reba had to cling to, right now.

"Fifteen minutes," he reported to her, when he'd finished the call. "You should lie down until they get here."

"Will that help?"

"Can't hurt."

"Can you call my friend Carla in? The red-haired waitress with the ponytail? I'd like to talk to her."

"Okay, I'll find her in a minute, when we've gotten you more comfortable." His mouth barely moved when he spoke, and his lips had thinned to two hard lines. "How many more weeks to go, Reba?"

"Fourteen."

Lucas didn't say a word to this, because there wasn't anything to say. He shaped his jacket into a make-shift pillow for her head and she lay on the carpet. He brought wads of paper towel to deal with the clear, innocent-seeming amniotic fluid, then he left the room to look for Carla.

While he was gone, two of those dull, ambiguous pains gave their sly squeeze to Reba's abdomen and her back, then slowly set her free again. She tried to tell herself that they weren't getting any stronger, any more regular, or any more defined.

But she was kidding herself.

Carla came in, knelt beside her, asked a couple of searching questions and told her, "You're doing the right thing. And the weather is holding off, so far. You want me to call your parents?"

"No, not yet. Please don't, Carla, I don't want them to worry."

"Let me stay with you, honey, till the ambulance gets here."

"It's okay. Go. I'll be all right. The place is a zoo tonight."

"You sure?"

"I'm sure."

Lucas and Carla passed each other in the doorway, no smiles exchanged, and Lucas dropped beside Reba again. He took both her hands in his and growled at her, "I'm sorry. I shouldn't have accused you of staging the miscarriage. I had no right."

"That's not important, now." But she was glad he'd said it, all the same.

His hands stayed folded around hers and she didn't try to push them away, because this wasn't the moment for that, not when their baby might be born tonight and might not survive.

Time passed like ice creeping down rock, until Reba and Lucas both heard the siren. Lucas leaped up and shot out of the office. Reba heard Gordie McConnell's voice out in the restaurant, cut off by another bark from Lucas. Gordie appeared in the doorway a moment later, white-faced.

"What's he done to you? I'll kill him!"

"Nothing."

"Maybe we should have gotten married, after all…"

"I'm telling you Gordon McConnell, that's not what I'm thinking about right now."

He kept standing there, shoring up the doorjamb, until the paramedics nudged him aside. They went through a couple of questions with her, but didn't waste much time. Getting wheeled on a gurney to the waiting vehicle, Reba felt several snowflakes on her face and thanked heaven that the fall was only light, hopefully not enough to slow them down on the hundred mile journey to Denver.

"What should I do?" Gordie's voice again. "Someone tell me."

Nobody did. Carla might have, if she'd overheard, but she would have been pretty blunt about it.

Instead Lucas told the paramedics, in a tone that invited no discussion, "I'll follow in my car," and the words gave Reba a rush of relief that left her weak to her bones.

She didn't know why she so badly wanted him with her, all of a sudden, when only half an hour ago she'd considered that he had no right to be involved, and when they'd been so hostile with each other. She just knew that she did want him—for his decisiveness, his strength, and most of all his primal biological connection to her unborn child.

"Which hospital are you headed for?" she heard him ask the paramedics.

"Rocky Mountain University Hospital, in Denver. It has a high-level neonatal intensive care unit. Are you related to the patient, sir?"

"I'm the baby's father."

In the background, Reba heard a woman shriek at this news.

At least Gordie didn't do the same. He was one of the few people who'd already known, as had Carla. Gordie's repeated offers to marry her "after all" had come prepackaged with the attitude that she'd owe him favors in return for the rest of her life, if he took on Lucas Halliday's child, and when she heard Carla's voice in the background telling Gordie just to please go home, she heartily hoped he'd stay there for the next month. No, forever.

One of the paramedics jumped into the driver's seat, while the other closed the rear doors and took her place beside Reba. "Any more contractions?" she asked.

"Another one, just then."

"Are they getting stronger?"

"I— Yes. Yes, they are."

"Hold on, okay? Safest way to transport a preemie baby is inside the mom."

"Won't the doctors be able to stop this?"

"You probably don't want them to, honey, not at this point, with your amniotic sac ruptured. The risk of infection and complications is too great."

Reba didn't ask any more questions after this, she just tried to relax and breathe, as the paramedic instructed, so that her baby would stay safe inside her all the way to Denver, more than a hundred miles through the falling snow.

Darkness and snow, frustration and fear.

The world narrowed to a tunnel of highway, slashed by the SUV's yellow headlights that seemed to catch each falling flake and fling it in Lucas's face. He'd never even gotten to order a meal at the steakhouse, let alone eat it, but hunger was the least of his concerns right now.

He had no clue what was happening inside the ambulance. He had followed it out of town, but it was travelling on full lights and sirens and he soon lost even the red glare of its taillights ahead of him.

Until they reached the Interstate, the snow on the road

made each tight bend treacherous, and every time he rounded one, he held his breath against the imagined sight of the ambulance piled and crumpled against a tree.

The Interstate was a stroll in the park by comparison, giving him time to experience a jarring sense of unreality when he thought about last September, and all the contrasts between then and now. Heat instead of cold, brilliant sun instead of darkness, his link with Reba one of sizzling, brazen, challenging desire, in place of the dragging fear he felt for her and the baby now.

The way they'd made love, the way they'd laughed and sparked off each other. Even the way they'd sometimes clashed had been a part of the attraction. Who knew it would lead to this? Who knew where it would go next, if their baby was born tonight?

Approaching Denver at last, after more than ninety minutes on the road, he realized he had no idea where Rocky Mountain University Hospital was. He pulled into a gas station, just off one of the last exits before the city. There, he filled up and bought a street map, which showed the large institution located several miles north of the downtown area, not far from where he currently was.

The stop had delayed him, and the ambulance must already have arrived, some minutes ago. Reba would have been hustled inside on a gurney, and taken…where? After finding a visitor's parking lot, parking the ranch pickup and negotiating the main reception desk, he knew only that he should "try the E.R.," because her name hadn't yet shown up on the computer data base.

By the time he got to her, she'd been taken to the Maternity floor because a doctor's examination had shown her to be in "established labor," so they made him put on a cap and gown.

"Does that mean…?" he asked her.

Reba nodded, voice expressionless and eyes too bright. "They're not going to try to stop it, and if it stops on its own, they'll give me something to keep it going. There's no possibility of the amniotic sac repairing itself. The baby has to be born, if it's to have any chance at life."

"What do you want me to do, Reba? Do you actually want me here? I—I never asked."

Her clammy hand locked around his forearm. "I want you here."

"Then I'm here."

Here. Stomach empty. Mind racing. Heart in his throat. Worst-case scenarios crowding his brain like gate-crashers at a party. A tenderness and terror for Reba and the baby that went beyond all logic or understanding. Yeah, he was here, and he wasn't going anywhere for a while.

He felt the moment when Reba's next contraction began, and he could tell instantly how much the pain had intensified since those moments in the manager's office at the steakhouse.

"What are they doing for you?" he asked. "Have they given you anything for the pain?"

"I don't want anything. I can handle it. I don't want this baby born drugged, on top of everything else."

She probably didn't need to feel that way. The staff wouldn't have offered her any medication that endangered the baby. But Lucas respected her attitude and didn't argue. This was happening to her body, not his.

Her body, but both their hearts.

A nurse appeared, wheeling some kind of preemie crash cart. He didn't know what to call it, but it looked scary, with its overhead lights, its instruments and equipment, and it brought home to him the reality of a baby who would need the most intensive level of care that a high-tech neonatal unit could provide. If he or she survived at all.

Time stretched and blurred.

The world narrowed to Reba's hand clutching his arm, her nails digging into his skin, her damp hair and her dry-mouthed cries. Her palms weren't callused the way they'd been last September, he vaguely noticed. Sometimes, she moved the same way she'd moved when they made love, but his memory of this snapped in and out of clarity so fast it felt like spots before his eyes.

When the time came for her to push the baby out, the room suddenly seemed to fill with people, all of them capped and gowned and masked in blue or green or white. They talked in a terse medical shorthand that seemed purposely designed to keep Lucas out of the loop, and he wanted to yell at them, "Tell me what's happening. Tell me what you're doing, and what that machine is for."

He was used to control, not this terrifying helplessness.

"Lucas…" Reba flung her head to one side, grabbed his arm even harder, then squared her body again, ready for the contraction that charged at her. She gave a tremendous heave.

"Beautiful!" someone said. "You're doing great, Rebecca. One more now. And… Yes!"

A flurry of action, more praise, as if from a coven of cheerleaders at some bizarre sporting event. A wet, wax-coated bundle, impossibly small, slipped into the hands of the waiting medical staff so fast Lucas didn't even see its face.

"She's a girl! You have a beautiful girl, Rebecca and Lucas."

A beautiful girl who wasn't breathing on her own.

After a pregnancy which had seemed to specialize in turning dramatic whenever Lucas was around, as if the universe was trying to send him a message he didn't want to hear.

A baby he'd felt ambivalent about, at best.

A tiny baby who'd been taken away, at once, into some secret corner of the room where the crash cart had been parked earlier, and where the gowned backs of the staff made a barrier Lucas couldn't see past. They muttered to each other, talked to the baby, too. Did that mean she was alive?

Lucas's own heart and lungs felt as if they'd hardened to stone. Of course the baby wasn't breathing! It hurt too damned much to breathe.

He felt no ambivalence now.

His eyes stung like acid burns, his jaw knotted and ached. Reba sobbed with exhaustion, still holding his arm, and gasped out, "Is she all right? Tell me she's all right!"

"Yes!" one of the doctors suddenly said. "Good girl!" He pumped the air with his fist.

"She's doing great!" said a nurse. She wasn't one of the people who'd been working on the baby, so how did she know?

Lucas felt the lightening of the atmosphere in the room, but didn't trust it. They were all still working frantically. What were they doing? He glimpsed IV lines and needles, heard a ripping sound. Tape?

Someone told Reba to "push gently with the contraction" and he vaguely realized that this must be the afterbirth. He leaned close to her. "Okay?"

"If she is." Her voice was shaky and squeaky and thin. "Can I see her? When can I see her?" she asked the nurse.

"Not yet, honey."

"Is she okay?"

"She's doing great."

Lucas still didn't believe it. It was too generic, too kind. He wanted facts and details. The baby's heart rate. Her blood pressure. Her weight. And he wanted to be told what it all meant.

Was she smaller or bigger than they'd expected? How bad was it that she hadn't breathed on her own? How many babies born fourteen weeks early survived? How many had problems? Were girls stronger than boys? He had an idea that they were.

A girl.

He was the father of a girl.

It didn't seem real, even though it felt so unexpectedly, earth-shatteringly important, and when the medical people wheeled the baby and that crash cart thing out of the room a little while later, he had a dizzying, terrifying sense that his daughter didn't exist any more, that he'd never see her again when he hadn't even really seen her in the first place.

Reba shared it, he could tell, and he didn't think he'd ever felt so linked to another human being, when just a few hours ago he'd considered that he barely knew her at all.

"Where is she?" She sounded tearful and panicky. "Where are they taking her?"

"She's gone up to the NICU, honey," said the nurse, who was still calmly fiddling around. "You'll be able to see her as soon as we've gotten you settled in your room. Do we have a name for her?"

"I had a few ideas. I wanted something strong, for a girl."

"Yes," Lucas heard himself say.

If the baby had a strong name, she'd be a strong person. She'd fight, and survive. The idea made a bizarre kind of sense, right now.

"Christie was one idea," Reba said. "Tara. Maggie."

"Maggie's good," Lucas said. "I like Maggie."

Reba turned to him, watched his face for a moment.

Reading him, it felt like. Reading his heart. "I like Maggie, too," she said.

"So she's Maggie?" the nurse asked. "Is she Margaret?"

"I think so, because that way she can shorten it to something different later on, if she wants."

"But for now she's Maggie."

"She's Maggie," Lucas agreed. He slipped his hand into Reba's and squeezed, and knew that for better or for worse, neither his life nor hers were ever going to be the same again.

"Is she going to be okay?"

The words just came out on their own. Reba knew they would only earn the same cautious reassurance she'd already heard more times than she could count, but there was only one thing in the world that mattered, right now, and that was Maggie being okay—her tiny daughter surviving and being okay—so she had to ask, and she had to endure the answer.

"She's doing real well, Rebecca," said the nurse, whose name was Shirley. She looked to be somewhere in her fifties, solidly built as if she'd given birth to several babies of her own. "She's looking good."

"Please call me Reba."

Because I know you're going to be in my life for weeks. And I *want* you to be in my life for weeks, because at best it's going to take weeks for Maggie to grow enough to go home. So we might as well get off to the right start with the name thing.

"Reba," the nurse repeated, with a smile.

She worked efficiently over the baby, checking monitors and making notes, trying only to invade the warmed interior of the isolette when she really had to. Reba had only been here in the NICU for a few minutes—she'd arrived in a wheelchair, pushed by a nurse—but the place had been Maggie's home for nearly two hours.

It still didn't seem real.

And where was Lucas?

He'd stayed with Reba until she was settled in her room, and then her nurse had suggested helping her through a shower before she was taken up to the NICU.

"There's paperwork I'm supposed to take care of, for you and the baby," he'd said at that point, his voice clipped and calm. "Let me get that out of the way while you're showering, and I'll meet you up there."

Sounded sensible in theory, but the paperwork seemed to be taking a long time.

What if he just didn't come back?

Watching her tiny baby, so vulnerable and so lost amongst tubes and tape and wires, so utterly precious with her black hair and crumpled face and miraculously moving chest, Reba felt Lucas's absence in a way that added hugely to her sense that none of this could actually, really, seriously be happening.

Finally, she heard a sound behind her, and felt his hand fall heavy and warm onto her shoulder. "She's so tiny," he said. "How can she be that small?"

"She's beautiful."

He looked at the baby for a moment, and Reba knew exactly what he was seeing. Thin, reddish limbs, a squashed face, hair like a black silk wig just fringing the edge of the pink knit hat that protected her fragile body heat. The hat was no bigger than a bone china teacup, but it looked like a sultan's outsized turban on Maggie's tiny head.

At first sight, you couldn't call her beautiful.

Still, Reba knew exactly the instant Lucas discovered

that she was. He drew in a hiss of breath, and a little sound caught in his throat and then escaped.

"She's stunning," he said. "She's fabulous." Then he turned to Shirley and said, "Is she going to be okay?"

Shirley gave the same reply she'd given Reba, then added, "Tell me, though, what can I smell? It's good…"

"Oh, right." He blinked, as if to clear his vision. "Are you hungry, Reba? I thought you might be, and that you should eat, but all I could find here at the hospital, at this hour, was a couple of vending machines. That's why I was gone so long. Found some takeout Chinese food, if you want it."

Hungry? Was she hungry?

Yes, Reba vaguely registered a gnawing, vinegary sort of sensation in her stomach that some people might label hunger, but it was so powerfully overlaid by, oh, about a hundred other, harder feelings, including the physical pain of recent childbirth, that it didn't seem important—until she looked at Maggie, who needed her mother to be strong, who might only *survive* if her mother stayed strong.

"Please," she said. "That was so— Thanks for thinking of it, Lucas."

"No problem. There you go."

And she plowed her way through countless mouthfuls of egg roll and fried rice that tasted like cardboard and salt but would help her to stay strong.

"I think I should try to sleep now," she said, some time later. Had to be three in the morning. Four, even. "Lucas, are you going to check into a motel for the rest of the night, or something?"

He shook his head impatiently, as if the question was a waste of his time. "I'll stay here."

He'd already asked Shirley a hundred questions, narrowing his tired eyes and nodding at her answers as if filing every fact and detail and scrap of information away like vital documents filed in a locked safe.

He hadn't sat down.

He'd asked if there were information booklets he could read, Internet sites he could look up, doctors he could talk to—as if Maggie's health and survival depended on him knowing everything there was to know about state-of-the-art preemie treatment, the way his business success depended on him knowing everything about a particular company or market trend.

It grated on Reba's red-raw nerves and she wanted to yell at him, "How is this going to help? Is this what our daughter really needs from you?"

But nobody yelled in the NICU, and she wouldn't yell at the father of her baby, who was *here,* when she hadn't had a clue, eight hours ago, just how much she would need him to be, and just how close to him she would feel.

"When are you heading back to New York?" she asked him, after he'd put the take-out containers in the garbage bin for her.

It was a little crazy, the way she didn't want him to go, how scared she was even to ask about it, how dark and unknowable her whole future seemed.

"Back to New York?" he echoed blankly, as if she'd asked the question in a foreign language.

"Yes. Or wherever. Back to your business commitments. How long are you staying in Denver, I should have said."

"Hell, Reba!" His voice harshened. "Weeks, if I have to. Until Maggie's doing better. Until she's—I can't think. Seems impossible to think beyond the next few hours."

"I know."

"But I'm in this with her as much as you are, and don't ever think you can turn me away."

Chapter Six

"Are you going to call your parents before you eat?" Lucas asked.

Bright Colorado morning sunshine flooded the private hospital room, helping Reba to wake up more fully, after four hours of broken sleep. She felt disoriented, desperate to see Maggie again and to hear the latest report from the baby's nurse, aware at the edge of her mind that there had to be all sorts of practical issues to deal with.

Lucas's question concerned one of them, and there was a phone right here beside her bed, so she couldn't argue the idea on grounds of inconvenience. It would be mid-morning in Florida by now.

But she shook her head in answer, and didn't make excuses. "I want to wait, not burden them with this. I don't want them worried. I want to have good news for them, first."

She struggled to sit up. There was a breakfast tray waiting for her and, again, she knew how important it was for her to eat. A nurse had poked her head around the door a few minutes ago, when she was still barely awake, wanting to talk to her about Maggie's nourishment, and how to provide breast milk for a baby who was way too little to suck. The whole idea seemed daunting, even when Reba knew how vital it was.

Lucas frowned at her and paced toward the window, half blocking the light. "You can't do that. How can you wait? Her birth is the best news they're going to get for a while."

"Is that right?" Her spirit prickled and rebelled at his tone. "How about you? Have you called yours?"

"I'm going to, later today. As soon as there's a window of time where I can think straight."

"We've each made our own decision, I guess."

"Is your decision a fair one? It could be weeks until we know for sure that she's going to be okay. They have a right to know as soon as possible, so they can make plans."

"Plans?"

"To see her, if they want."

"I don't want Mom burdened like that, when her health is so precarious."

"It's not your call, Reba." He hunched shoulders that were already tight with tension and fatigue, but she couldn't think about his body language, only about what he'd just said.

"If we're talking about rights, what gives you the right to dictate to me, the way you're doing?"

"I'm not dictating to you, I'm talking about what's the right thing to do."

"In your opinion."

"This isn't about opinions, it's about principles."

"Which you're the expert on, appa—appa—apparently." She didn't really know why they were arguing, but finally got the word out at her third squeaky try, and suddenly she was in tears, as if an emotional floodgate had opened inside her.

Lucas came to her at once and enfolded her into an embrace that smelled like coffee and soap and warmth, and felt as solid and safe as the trunk of a tree. "Hey…" he said. "Hey, Reba, it's okay. I'm not going to put a gun in your back and march you to the nearest phone. Not today."

"Oh, but tomorrow, maybe?"

He said nothing for a moment, clearly struggling to stay in control, which didn't trouble Reba because it would be good for him to know how that kind of a struggle felt. She doubted he would *ever* know how it felt to be unable to stop crying like this.

"Think about it, okay?" he suggested finally, in a neutral, wooden tone. "It's important."

"Baby blues," said the lactation nurse, appearing again.

"It's not!" Reba said, through her sobs. "It's much more real than that!"

The nurse clicked her tongue and said mildly, "I never said it wasn't real, honey."

This didn't help.

"Listen, I've checked us into a hotel suite, five minutes from here." Lucas's voice vibrated deep into Reba's body, and she calmed a little as she listened to him. "It's an open-ended reservation. The place has twenty-four-hour room service and a business center and a pool."

"We need a pool?"

"We need a nice place. And I'm wondering how we can get some of our things down here, so we don't have to make the drive up to Biggins ourselves. Is there a friend who has a key to your place and can fill a couple of suitcases for you? Carla? Then one of the hands at the ranch can pick them up and bring them down, along with my gear."

"You're really staying?"

"You're trying to exclude me, as well as your parents?"

"I'm not excluding anyone." The idea seemed too unfair—unfair that he'd suggested it, unfair of her to even contemplate doing it, which, to be honest, she had—and she cried some more, silently daring the poor lactation nurse to mention those words "baby blues" again.

"I'm staying, Reba," Lucas said. "I'm not leaving you alone to deal with this. And I'm not leaving our baby."

"Okay." This one tiny word couldn't begin to express the strength and mix of emotions she felt at what he'd said, but then a whole dictionary couldn't have done that. "Thank you."

"Don't thank me. I'm— It's not about that."

"You said you'd already checked in. Oh, and yes, Carla has a key," she interrupted herself, her mind darting so much she'd get dizzy in a minute. "Have you slept, yet?"

"Later." No wonder he looked tired, then. "Let's get our priorities in place, first."

Seeing Maggie was priority one, as soon as Reba had eaten and made her first questionable attempt at producing something from her uncooperative and increasingly heavy breasts. She had another cry, and got dressed in yesterday's clothes, while Lucas waited patiently in the corridor outside. It wasn't until she'd put on her sneakers and socks that she realized everything was dry and clean and pressed and fresh.

"Laundry service at the hotel," Lucas said, when she asked.

"Thank you, from the bottom of my heart."

"You're welcome. And you can cry again, if you want," he offered—belatedly, because she already was.

Maggie.

Maggie.

Maggie.

Reba didn't cry any more once they got to the Neonatal Unit, because this tiny, fragile baby girl of theirs was just too important for hormonal tears. "Is she doing better?"

"As well as she knows how, honey." This wasn't Shirley, because her shift had ended. This was Angela, whose name and face needed to be learned by heart, too, because she would be just as important.

Angela had flyaway mouse-blond hair, and fine wrinkles around her eyes, and wore plum-colored scrubs. She didn't look as motherly as Shirley, but she darted around, as neat as a bird.

"She's lost weight," Lucas said, studying a chart that was already several pages thick.

Reba didn't want to look at all that scribble from different doctors and nurses and infant respiratory therapists, when she hadn't known that infant respiratory therapists existed twenty-four hours ago. Lucas, however, studied it like a *Star Trek* nut trying to learn Klingon.

This bothered her, even angered her, but she didn't know why so she tried to ignore it.

"She weighed 940 grams at birth," he went on, "but now she's dipped down to below nine hundred."

"They all lose weight, even healthy babies born at term," Angela said.

"But she's already so tiny." He shook his head. "She can't afford to lose any more. Can she? When does it stop? When does she start coming back up? What do you do if she doesn't?"

"That depends on a whole lot of things. Do you want to write down some of your questions, Lucas, so you can ask

Maggie's neonatologist? He's going to want to talk to you this morning."

"Questions," Lucas muttered. He asked for pen and paper and began to cover it with his confident scrawl.

Reba didn't contribute. She just sat, trying to ignore Lucas scribbling as if undertaking a major written exam.

"Can I touch her?" she said softly to Angela, after a few moments.

Lucas kept writing.

"She'll love that, if you do it right," the nurse answered. "She needs to know that touching feels good, because we've done too much bad touching to her, since she was born." She dropped her voice to a soothing coo, and spoke directly to the baby. "We hated it, didn't we, Maggie-baby? We didn't want to do any of it. But you needed it. We're going to try our best not to do so much of that, now, if you'll help us a little bit by staying strong."

"Oh, sweetheart!" Reba whispered. "Angela, you'll have to tell me what to do, how to do it exactly right."

The older nurse coached her through the process of washing her hands up to her elbows, sliding one arm through the ports of the isolette and curving her hand around and beneath the baby's tiny bottom and curled up legs. No stroking, no squeezing, just a firm steady hold that mimicked the reassuring pressure Maggie had experienced from Reba's own uterine muscles, less than twenty-four hours ago.

Her neck and shoulder soon grew stiff because she hadn't gotten herself in quite the right position first, but it felt so good to be touching Maggie that she never wanted to move, and after a while, Angela said softly to her, "See what you're doing? Look at the way her oxygen saturation has gone up on the monitor. And look at her color. It's more even, now, and it's that nice pink we love to see. She loves this."

"She does?"

"You can see it. She's not twitching the way she was."

"I haven't heard her cry. Has she cried much?"

"She can't cry, honey. She has the breathing tube between her vocal cords."

"Doesn't that hurt her?"

"Well, it doesn't feel great, no, but she needs it to help her breathe."

"I wish I could explain that to her."

"I know. You want to do so much more for her, don't you?"

"I just want her to be okay. And to hold her. When will we be able to hold her?"

"We're going to have to wait a while on that, I'm afraid. She's just too small and frail, right now, with too many lines and monitors in place. The doctor will okay it when he thinks she's ready. It might be two or three weeks. Just touching her is best."

"When can we see the doctor?" Lucas said, looking up from his page of questions. He frowned across at Reba and looked suspiciously at the curve of her hand around Maggie as if he didn't trust its beneficial effect.

"He's just finishing a procedure on another baby at the other end of the unit," Angela said. "He'll come by in a minute, and then you can take some time with him in our conference room, if you want."

"Yep. Thanks."

A big part of Reba wished that she could stay with Maggie, just keep holding her and watching the pink color and the high oxygen saturation and the nice, relaxed look to her limbs, all of which she now knew to be important. But it was important to talk to the doctor, too.

His name was Dr. Phil Charleson. He had a bushy head of dark hair and wire-framed glasses and he listened to their concerns with as much focus as even Lucas, with his page of demanding questions, could have wanted.

He also told them, "There are several dangers we'll be watching out for. Respiratory problems, heart problems, gut problems, bleeding, infection. We've got a whole lot better, in recent years, at ironing those things out and at preventing them in the first place, but this little girl is very small and fragile and I'm not going to make promises to you that we might not be able to keep."

"We understand that," Lucas answered for them both.

He hadn't touched Reba since moving into this little conference room, and she felt very distant from him right now, very separate and at odds, way too wrapped up in her body and her fears to remember a connection with him that she'd never understood, even while it was happening.

They barely knew each other.

About the only thing they were doing for each other, right now, was loving the same fragile child, and coexisting in the same space.

"I don't understand it!" she wanted to yell, in contradiction to Lucas's reasoned words. "I do want promises! How can I get through this without promises?"

But she stayed silent and tried to accept that false promises might hurt even worse, down the track. Her body ached and stung following the jarring labor of giving birth, and her breasts tingled every time she thought a new thought about Maggie.

"Can we visit whenever we want?" Lucas asked, and she pricked up her ears, because in the middle of his long interrogation about the monitors and the equipment and the medication and the treatment philosophy, this was one question she wanted an answer to as much as he did.

"Yes, you can," Dr. Charleson said. "We try to maintain defined quiet periods in the unit, but you'll get to know when those are, and you can still be with your baby, any hour of any day. You're cleared for discharge today, Reba?"

"I haven't seen the obstetrician, yet, but the nurse seemed to think so, this morning."

"And we have your contact details?"

She was about to shake her head, but Lucas said, "Yes, I've fixed all that up." She was grateful for that.

"In case we need to call you when you're not around," Dr. Charleson finished.

Neither of them liked the sound of that. Lucas laced his fingers through hers and squeezed, and she squeezed back, flooded with a relief, once again, that he was here, that she wasn't alone, as she so easily might have been.

"Be good to each other," Dr. Charleson said.

He probably thought they were married, or at least seriously involved.

They weren't, but they had Maggie, joining them together in shared love and fear like two links in a steel chain. What sort of a bond would this turn out to be? Since she could hardly think beyond the next hour, Reba had no idea.

The hotel Lucas had chosen was beautiful. Situated next to a golf course and surrounded by pampered gardens, it seemed like an oasis that existed in a different universe to the nearby hospital, with its aura of life-altering drama. The spacious lobby was quiet and cool and attractively lit. It led to two restaurants and a bar, as well as to the bank of elevators that traveled to the higher floors.

Their suite was almost at the top of the building, and featured a huge marble bathroom, a powder room, a vast master bedroom, and a sitting room with a king-size pull-down Murphy bed, fresh flowers in vases and a fully stocked bar fridge.

Reba had never stayed in a place like this in her life, and wasn't exactly in the mood to take maximum advantage of its luxury, right now. She did appreciate the bar fridge and the twenty-four-hour room service, because she'd probably need snacks and meals at odd hours.

And she appreciated the clean, smooth expanse of the bed, and the fact that there was a second bed in the sitting room, because she and Lucas might have created a child together but that said nothing about the state of their relationship now, six months later.

The obstetrician had commented on her relatively easy delivery, in terms of its effect on her own body, and had issued what was clearly a standard prohibition on marital relations "for at least two weeks, and then only if you feel ready" and Reba had just nodded, keeping the state of her private life to herself.

"The bedroom's yours, obviously," Lucas said, as if his thoughts had travelled in exactly the same direction. "And you should sleep for a couple of hours, before we head back to the hospital."

"So should you."

"I'm fine. I need to call the ranch and get Lon on the road with our gear."

"I'll call Carla and ask if she can pack a couple of bags for me. Lon can meet her at my house."

"After you've napped, call your parents."

"Don't tell me how to handle this, Lucas."

"They have a right to know. They'll want to know.

Even though it's not a piece of news they'd ever have chosen to hear."

Reba remained stubbornly silent. She didn't want to call Mom and Dad while she still felt so tearful, in case she sobbed down the phone and got them really alarmed. If they felt they had to jump on a plane, when she knew her mother had been feeling pretty bad these past few weeks...

"Was lunch enough for you, at the hospital?" Lucas asked, after a minute.

"It was fine. I don't feel hungry."

"Take that nap, then we'll order something from room service before we head back."

She began to bristle at the fact that he was giving her orders again, but he must have seen it, because suddenly he'd stepped closer—close enough to brush a strand of hair back from her face and curve a hand around her hip.

"Hey," he said. "I'm not being a control freak, here."

"No?" She lifted her chin and glared at him, felt his usual onslaught on her senses. It charged through her like electricity, and threatened to knock her sideways.

That's right.

I remember now.

This.

"Tell me this hasn't been the hardest eighteen hours of your life, and I'll back off," he said softly. "Can you tell me that? I doubt it."

"Don't make me cry again!"

"I just want you to look after yourself, that's all. Maggie needs you. And you and I are in this together, aren't we? For her sake? Till she's healthy and growing and ready to go home?"

"The doctor wouldn't make promises," she reminded him, her voice shaky.

"It's not about promises, it's about faith. We have to believe in her. We have to believe in ourselves. Believe that the way we feel about her can make a difference. Are we being fair to her if we fight about things like taking naps and calling people?"

Okay, here come the tears again…

"I'm just a mess today, that's all. And of course it's baby blues. And I hate that. Being a victim of my body and my hormones and—I should be stronger than that, shouldn't I, for Maggie?"

"Sometimes it's strongest to let yourself cry, sweetheart," he whispered.

She felt his arms, heard him shushing her the way he would one day, please God, shush Maggie when she cried. He coaxed her head down to his shoulder and even though sobs still shook her body, she closed her eyes and drank in the nutty, fragrant smell of his neck, where the skin curved down from his hairline, fine and brown, to disappear inside the collar of his shirt.

It helped.

He helped, caring enough to hold her close like this.

He helped more than she wanted to think about, and more than she wanted him to know.

"I'll take that nap, now," she said finally, many minutes later.

Lucas called his parents while Reba was asleep and, yeah, it was hard. Harder than he'd allowed, when he and Reba had had those…uh…*heated discussions,* you could call them…about the principles involved. If he hadn't believed so strongly that it was the right thing to do, he might have put it off, himself, because how did you find the right words?

Mom was the one blessed with his first attempt, after

he'd keyed in the phone number of the high-end fashion boutique she owned in Beverly Hills.

Guess what, Mom, I'm a father, when neither you nor I knew that the woman involved was even pregnant. And guess what, the baby's seriously premature and might not make it, so the fatherhood thing may not last for long. Which would at least make the question of my future relationship with the baby's mother a little less complicated.

Somehow, he stumbled through those basic facts, and somehow his mother managed to cut to the heart of it and ask the right questions.

"What's her name? Does she look strong? Is she likely to have ongoing problems? And her mom? Reba, you said? Is she handling it? This is going to be a very tough time for her. Can you make sure that she knows how much I'll be thinking of her?"

His answers were sketchy, cutting off in midsentence and starting again, filled with pauses and struggles for the right word.

"Do you want me on the next plane?" Mom asked finally.

"I want you to do what you need to do, as Maggie's grandmother."

"No," his mother said decisively, in answer to this. "It's not about me. It's about the three of you, and from what you've said, I'm sure Reba, at least, would appreciate a little more time before she has to deal with a grandmother to her baby that she's never met. And if my son needs a shoulder to cry on…"

"Yes?"

"It should be hers. Reba's."

"Mom, we—"

"For now, at least, even if you go your separate ways just a few months from now. For Maggie's sake. No, you know I want to come, but I'm not going to until you tell me it's okay for Reba."

He reached his father next, after getting routed through three secretaries in three different Halliday corporate offices. Dad was in Dallas this week, it turned out.

"Sounds like a mess," he said, even though Lucas's announcement had been worded just a little less messily, this time around.

"We're hoping it doesn't have to be," he told his father.

"I'd like to see her. My first grandchild. But not until her doctors are sure she's going to make it. If I see her, I'll get attached. I'm not making that investment."

"Your call, Dad."

He knew he sounded cool, and his father picked up on it, of course.

"Well, I'm calling it as I see it," Farrer Halliday said, without a hint of apology. "And don't conclude that I'm being cold and unfeeling. The reverse. I'm a parent. I've been there. This stuff hurts. I'm not going to get hurt if I don't have to. So you'll let me know when I should come. When it's...safe."

Scary word. It didn't really succeed in skirting the dark possibility that his father didn't want to refer to in direct language.

"I'll let you know," Lucas answered. "Want progress reports, until then?"

His father was silent. Then he sighed. And swore. "Of course I want progress reports. I'll *need* them like I need a hole in the head. But I want them. Sometimes humans just don't know what's good for them, do they?"

"No," Lucas answered. "Sometimes they don't."

Chapter Seven

"**M**om?" Reba said, when she heard the familiar voice at the far end of the line.

"Hi, honey, how are you?"

"First, how are you? You're up and about, for a start, and that's good." Reba knew her mother only answered the phone when she felt comparatively well.

"Feeling better, these past few days."

"I'm sorry I haven't called this week. I have some news, Mom."

Don't cry, don't cry, don't cry.

You shouldn't still be crying this much. Maggie is three and a half days old, and she hasn't had any setbacks, yet. Your milk has come in, and you're managing to fill those little glass bottles the nurses keep giving you—sometimes. Maggie needs you to handle all of this, so get over yourself.

"It's pretty hard," Reba managed to add.

She told her mother about Maggie's birth, then heard her father pick up the extension, and had to re-cap and fill in details. It was a confused, emotional conversation, and that awful crying was tough to keep at bay. She hardly registered the click of the door at the far end of the suite, as Lucas let himself in.

"No, Mom, I'm not letting you fly all this way. Not yet. She's too little to hold. She may not even— She's…fragile. Wait until she's stronger. Until the weather's warmer here."

"That long?" Mom sounded teary, too.

"She's going to be in the hospital for weeks and weeks."

Dad said, "We'll talk it over, Reba. We don't like to think of you on your own."

"I'm not on my own. Lucas is here."

She'd told her parents about the father of her baby months ago, when she'd first realized she was pregnant, but had warned them there was no likelihood of a future between Lucas and herself, despite the fact that his family's corporation had bought Seven Mile. Mom and Dad had been so good about it. No judgments. No negative questions. Just care and concern.

"He flew in?" Dad asked now.

"He was out at the ranch. He came into town, and— The details aren't important, right now. We'll talk about all that later. But it meant that he was here, and he wants to stay. For Maggie's sake. Until she's well and strong. We'll have a lot to talk about, and to work out. We're not ready to think about any of that yet. But I want you to stay put in Florida until everything's—until I tell you it's okay to come, all right? That's all I'm asking from you, right now."

"Well, if that's really what you want, honey, we'll respect it," her father said. "I know you're concerned about your mother."

"Look after yourself," Mom put in. "Call us every day, if you can, because we're going to be sitting by the phone."

"I'll call. Just don't worry, okay. I love you. Bye."

Reba put down the phone and looked across the room to find Lucas watching her in silence. She expected a repetition of his insistence, three days ago, that her parents should make their own decision about coming to Colorado to see Maggie, and steeled herself to put a lock on the subject. She wouldn't hesitate to tell him again to butt out, if it came to the point.

She might actually tell him to butt out right now, before he even opened his mouth!

But no.

No.

What was that look on his face?

Her stomach suddenly dropped and she levered herself off the edge of the bed, her strength gone in an instant. "What's happened? I thought you must be getting breakfast, but—have you been at the hospital?"

"No, I've been—" He cut off, as if the explanation was irrelevant. "The doctor called while you were still asleep, Reba. They want to talk to us about her heart."

Reba's hands shook so much as she dressed that she could hardly fasten the buttons on her shirt. The tears that fogged her vision didn't help. Neither did the sound of Lucas pacing impatiently near the door, waiting for her. Striding toward the elevator, he moved so fast that she would have had to run to keep up. Would have *wanted* to run, too, but she was still a little sore and cautious in her movements, following the birth, so she kind of loped along, like a wounded rabbit.

In the lobby, he peeled away from the direction of the

exit and she followed him instinctively, then couldn't believe it when he disappeared through the door of the hotel's business center.

"Lucas?" she almost yelled. "You're trading stocks, or something, when Maggie might be—?"

But she knew she'd gotten it wrong the moment he turned and she saw his bleak face. Heard his tight tone, also. "After the doctor called, I came down here and went on the Internet to see what more I could find out. He didn't say much about it over the phone."

"Oh. Right." Reba felt as if her throat had been gripped by a metal clamp.

"Mr. Halliday?" said a cool-voiced office assistant.

"Yes?" He whipped around to face her. "Is everything printed out?"

"Here it is." The woman gave a professional smile and handed him a manila file filled with printed sheets. It had to be an inch thick.

"All that?" Reba said. "That's all related to Maggie's heart?"

"It's information on preemies in general, and on the condition she has—*patent ductus arteriosus*—from about ten or twelve different sites," Lucas answered. "They seem reputable. A couple are run by children's hospitals, one by a neonatology association."

Standing close and holding the file folder so she could see, he flipped it open to a random page, where Reba saw the stylized diagram of a preemie baby's heart. He flipped again, and weird words jumped out at her.

Ventriculomegaly.

Subependymal.

Parenchmyal hemorrhage.

Hemorrhage was the only one she recognized, the only

one she would even try to pronounce, and it meant bleeding. Was Maggie bleeding?

"I don't want to look," she told Lucas, close to total panic. "What's the point of this? I only want to hear what the doctor thinks we need to know. Or it'll just get me more scared."

"The doctor didn't say much. I wanted some background on this—factual, detailed medical background—so I know what to ask."

"Okay. That's your choice. Can we just get to the hospital now and see her? Find out?"

Morning traffic was still thick on the roads and their vehicle seemed to crawl. At one point they came to a complete standstill, and to cool his impatience Lucas pulled yet another sheet from the manila file and frowned at it as he read, saying nothing. Reba wanted to scream. She also wanted to grab the printouts from his hands, crumple them and hurl them out the window.

Something about the way he needed to tackle the morning's news rubbed her raw, but when the traffic started moving again and she looked across at him and saw the way he kept raking his lower lip with his teeth, the way his hands were so tense on the wheel, she could see her own fear mirrored in every strung-out movement he made, and every new line on his face.

When she saw all this, suddenly, she wanted to reach out to him, soothe that tight face with her fingers, massage his neck and give him all the promises that Maggie's doctor had refused to make.

It seemed hours before they reached the unit, and then to torture them further, Dr. Charleson wasn't there.

"He's in the delivery suite right now," Angela told them. "He'll be back as soon as he can."

"How is she?"

"She's doing great."

"Angela, please stop saying that," Reba begged. "We know she has a heart condition. Lucas had a call from Dr. Charleson."

"A lot of preemies have this condition. Before birth, the heart doesn't need to pump much blood through the heart, so there's a kind of in-built by-pass. In a full-term baby—a baby who's born at the right time—it closes after birth, but sometimes in preemies it doesn't. It's not regarded as a defect, honey, not in the same way as some other conditions."

"But it'll need treatment."

"It's starting to look that way. He's put her on some medication, and—"

"Not just medication. I've done some reading," Lucas cut in. "She may need surgery."

"Please wait until Dr. Charleson can talk to you about that. Yes, she may need surgery, but she may not."

Surgery on a baby this small.

Heart surgery.

Looking down at Maggie, Reba couldn't even imagine it. How delicate must such a tiny heart be! How minuscule were its blood vessels? And how would Maggie's precious little body withstand an invasion like that, even if it was intended to save her life?

Lucas made a sound that could have been an oath, or a rusty sob. He scraped his teeth across his bottom lip again, and his shoulders hunched up as if Angela's reassuring words and her relaxed way of moving around Maggie had sent his blood pressure shooting through the roof without any input from Dr. Charleson.

"Have you guys eaten this morning?" Angela said, a moment later.

"Uh…" Lucas looked at Reba.

"I haven't, no."

"Me, neither." His voice rasped. "I'll get us coffee and Danish, Reba, okay?"

"Could I have an orange juice, too. A banana, if you can." Keeping her vitamins up for Maggie, giving Maggie strength through her milk.

"Sure," Lucas said. "Back ASAP."

He left the unit, his big body all angles and thrusts as it moved, and Angela pulled up a chair for Reba. "Sit, honey."

Maggie's color didn't appear so good this morning. Reba looked at the monitors and saw that the baby's oxygen settings were higher than they had been last night—a fact she wouldn't even have recognized just three days ago.

"How did Dr. Charleson pick up the heart condition, Angela?" she asked.

"He heard a murmur through the stethoscope. That's not necessarily significant, but she's needed more breathing support since last night and her heart rate has climbed a little. When that happened, they gave Maggie an echocardiogram—it didn't hurt her, it's just sound waves, the same principle as the ultrasound you would have had during pregnancy—and then he knew for sure."

"Right. I understand."

Okay.

It was time.

Reba knew she had to ask the question that had tortured her since the moment she'd realized there was no stopping her labor and her baby was going to be born, three agonizing days ago.

She took a breath, and her voice came out steady. "Did I make all this happen?"

Angela's hand stilled over the sheet of medical notes she

was adding to, and she looked across the baby's isolette at Reba. "You mean, was it your fault that Maggie came early?"

"Yes."

"Well, honey, did you go out parachuting the day before? Bungee jumping, maybe? Did you have a drinking binge or take cocaine?"

Reba gave a shaky laugh. "No!"

"Didn't think you looked the type for any of that. Now look at me, and read my lips. No, you didn't make it happen."

"I—I kept working, though. I did five shifts a week as a short-order cook at our local steakhouse. I was there—I was working—when my waters broke."

"Plenty of women keep working in physically demanding jobs right up until the birth with no problems. Some women push their luck in all sorts of ways and breeze through the whole pregnancy and birth. Others, like you, do everything right—right diet, right exercise—and have a truckload of complications. It's not fair."

"Feels pretty unfair, right now, for sure!"

"But it's most definitely not your fault."

"I was feeling pretty stressed, though. A lot of stuff was happening. When the miscarriage happened a few months ago, and when I went into labor."

"And stress is your fault, too, right? *Life* is your fault." Angela pretended to raise her voice, and grinned as she spoke. "Hey, everyone, good news, we've found her, the woman we can blame for everything. Traffic. Floods. Bad TV."

Reba laughed again, although from the outside it might have looked more like crying. "I get your point."

"Don't burden yourself with guilt, along with everything else you're dealing with, okay? Just don't. Promise?"

"I promise to try."

Lucas came back a few minutes later, and they ate breakfast in the parents' room just outside the unit. Dr. Charleson found them as they were finishing their coffee.

"Don't skimp on the details," Lucas warned him, hard on the heels of the brief greetings they exchanged. "Don't give us the soft version, okay? I want all of it, and I want it straight."

What if I don't? Reba wondered. What if I'm not strong enough for that? Do I get a choice?

She almost spoke out in protest, but then she felt Lucas's arm dropping around her shoulders and his hip and thigh against her side. He squeezed her close, his chest shoring her shoulder blade, and she leaned her head back to pillow against the pad of muscle just below his collar bone. His fresh scent enveloped her and she could almost feel his strength seeping into her pores, making her just a little stronger, too.

For Maggie's sake, they were in this together and she wasn't going to argue her own weakness in front of their baby's doctor.

"Yes," she said, swallowing what she felt. "Please give us the whole story, Dr. Charleson, as clearly as you can."

"How long before you'll know if she needs the surgery?" Lucas asked. He felt as if they'd been closeted in the parents' room with their baby's doctor for hours, but it was probably closer to ten minutes.

He still held Reba, her willowy body positioned against his right side and chest. He could feel the way she was breathing—almost the same way she'd breathed through labor, as if the deliberate, conscious action of expanding and contracting her lungs was the only thing stopping her whole body from flying apart.

He knew how much she didn't want to hear any of this, how much she just wanted to be told the punchline to Fate's latest cruel joke. But he knew there was no punchline, yet, so they had to hear about all the ifs and buts, the wait and sees, the let's hopes, the worst-case scenarios.

He'd first held her in order to help her through all of this, but within seconds he lost track of who was helping whom. He might be stronger than her physically, and he might possess more outward fight, but the touch of her and the warmth of her gave back to him just as much as he gave out. He wanted her, needed her, valued her.

And he wondered how they'd feel about each other when all this was over, when Maggie was out of danger and ready to go home. Would they be friends? Or would their teeth set on edge every time they had to be in the same room?

He knew he wasn't prepared to let Maggie out of his life, whether she was strong and healthy and normal or...not. How would he and Reba work it out?

Please God, let us get safely to that problem, don't let those decisions get taken out of our hands by something worse...

"Definitively, how long?" Dr. Charleson said, in answer to his question. "By the time she's a couple of weeks old."

He sketched out a possible scenario—that the drugs they were giving Maggie to close the open ductus in her heart would appear to work, but then the hole would open again after a few days without medication. They'd try a second course of medication at that point, and if they had the same failure, they'd then move on to the surgical option.

"Is she in danger if you wait?" Reba asked.

"We'll have to work harder at supporting her breathing and her heart, while the ductus remains open, yes. If you consider that this increased support can also lead to increased chances of various other problems, then I'd have to say—I can't soften this for you—there could be consequences. A ripple effect."

"And if you don't wait, if you decide to perform the surgery now?"

"We're not going to do that. The medication is a better option. We're going to cross our fingers that it works."

"Crossing your fingers?" Lucas repeated. "Latest medical technique?"

"Sometimes, it's all we've got. I will tell you, though, that I'm very optimistic on this one. She's responded well to the medication so far. We'll know within twenty-four hours whether the hole has closed." Dr. Charleson looked at his watch, then added, "I'm not rushing you, please ask any questions you have, but if you're okay with what we've discussed, I will get back to another newborn I'm concerned about."

"We're fine," Reba answered quickly. "Thank you. We have no more questions right now."

When the neonatologist had left the room a few moments later, Lucas said to her, only half teasing, "Afraid of what I was going to ask next?"

For some seconds, she didn't answer, then said finally, "Do you like roller coasters, Lucas?"

"Nope."

"Neither do I. Not even for one three-minute ride. Now we're both strapped to the front of the lead car, and the ride isn't going to stop for weeks."

"And you want to close your eyes?"

"No, closing your eyes is worse. I just want to put my hand in front of my face and peek when I have the courage, to get an idea of what's coming. Since there's no way to get off."

"Whereas I'm gripping the bar with white knuckles,

while trying to calculate the angles of force and the breaking strain on the car couplings?"

"Something like that."

"Do you recommend your own approach?"

"I don't think either of us has a choice. We are who we are. Don't you think? We're not going to change."

The statement seemed designed to stress the distance that divided them, and Lucas didn't like it. Was that really what she meant? He'd felt pretty close to her since Maggie's birth, like they were on the same team. Now he wondered if Reba saw their tentative connection breaking down, sometime soon.

She would know, as he did, that the stress of something like this could break even a close, loving couple apart. A lot of marriages failed when there was a baby with special needs in the family. And he and Reba hadn't had any kind of a foundation in the first place. Not a marriage, not even an ongoing involvement.

Statistically the odds couldn't possibly be in their favor.

Chapter Eight

Lucas appeared to be fast asleep, his big body dwarfing the uncomfortable upright chair he was sprawled in, beside the baby's isolette. Reba wondered if he'd been sleeping like that all night.

He'd sent her back to the hotel from the hospital at ten yesterday evening, after they'd grabbed a meal together in the hospital dining room. Already, she couldn't remember what they'd eaten. Pasta? Or was that what she'd had for lunch? The indifferent cuisine blurred together after a while—overcooked glop that she ate purely to keep body and soul in one piece.

Had Lucas come into their suite later, when she was already asleep?

Probably not.

She certainly hadn't heard him, and surely she would have done, because she hadn't slept well. Now, she could see the darkening of new beard growth on his chin and jaw, and his hair had begun to look overdue for a trim. His muscles must ache from his twisted posture in the chair, his eyes must feel gritty and his clothing stale.

She knew all this, because she'd slept a couple of nights in that chair herself, although Lucas refused to let her do it very often. "If exhaustion dries up your milk…" Probably the only argument in the world that he could have gotten her to accept.

Maggie would be two weeks old tomorrow.

Reba had counted each day like counting precious pearls on a string. Their baby had survived another precious day. She'd gotten even more beautiful to Reba's gaze. She'd tolerated a barrage of medications and all the noise and touch and treatments that stressed her immature nervous system. She'd put on a few precious grams of weight.

Precious, precious, precious.

If Reba had had only her own body to consult, however, she wouldn't have had a clue about the days. Like the hospital meals, they'd all blurred, as had the phone calls she and Lucas had both made regularly to their families, to keep them posted on Maggie's progress, as had the sheets and sheets and books and books of information about preemies that Lucas had gathered.

Reba looked at these sometimes, drawn to them like a moth to a flame, even though she knew that too much information only threatened the fragile hold she had on her emotional control. Lucas seemed to draw something positive from them, but she couldn't.

How did it help to learn that a baby born at twenty-six weeks gestation had a twenty-eight percent chance of dying, and a forty percent chance of needing medical or surgical treatment for a scary thing called necrotizing enterocolitis? How did it help to read the true stories of other preemies, even when those stories ended happily?

A couple of events stood out from the mist. Reba had had her one-week postpartum check-up and everything was fine. Maggie had had a course of treatment with a special blue "bili" light because her body had turned yellow with jaundice, which they were told was very common in preemies and not a cause for concern. And she had come off her first course of the medication to close her open heart ductus, which had encouraged Reba and Lucas to risk a cautious celebration.

A pay-per-view movie and take-out pizza in their suite, with a surprising amount of laughter and connection in the mix.

Woo-hoo!

But even that had turned to ash a couple of days later, when the hole in the heart had opened again and Maggie had been put back on her medication—another series of three doses, through her IV line, over the course of twenty-four hours. This second course had been given five days ago, and when Reba saw Lucas keeping such an uncomfortable vigil in the chair her whole gut lurched.

Had he stayed all night because he knew something Reba didn't? Had the hole opened again? Was Maggie facing surgery, now?

Where was Shirley? This should still be her shift, not Angela's. Okay, here she was, coming toward this little corner of the unit with her usual comfortable gait. She must have snatched a bathroom break.

Not wanting to disturb Lucas or Maggie, Reba went to meet the nurse. "How has she been, overnight? Has Dr. Charleson seen her since yesterday afternoon?"

"He dropped by at around midnight."

Reba tried to laugh. "Does that man ever go home?"

"His wife sure doesn't think so," Shirley shot back, then added more seriously "No, he was on call, and we had some drama, but not over Maggie."

"So her heart hasn't opened up again?"

"No, she's doing great. Her levels are good. Dr. Charleson was pleased."

"So Lucas stayed all night just because…?"

"Because he can't stay away, honey. He has to stay on top of everything, at every moment. Some parents are like that."

"I don't understand it. And I don't see how you can act so calm about it. Seems like he's practically shouting that he doesn't trust you."

Shirley shrugged and smiled. "We've seen it before."

"Does that mean I'm burying my head in the sand because I don't want to know every detail?"

"No. You're taking care of yourself, in your own way. Getting the rest you need, I'm hoping."

"I'm only doing it for Maggie, because of the milk."

Maggie wasn't even taking the milk, yet. Her tiny digestive system hadn't matured enough. She was still on nutrition fed directly into her veins and the stump of her cord. But she'd be ready for the milk soon, if she continued to progress, and so Reba had to make sure it was available. She stored sterilized jars of it in the hotel suite's bar fridge whenever she was there, and ferried them to the neonatal unit's freezer each day, and every one of those jars was the product of an hour of effort and frustration.

"You should be doing it for your own sake. And so should Lucas," Shirley said. She dropped her voice below the murmuring pitch they were both using. "It would be great if you could get him to take some time out."

"I doubt he'd listen…"

"A man who does what he wants?"

"A man who owns his whole universe, I think."

"That would fit."

Yes, it would. She'd known this about Lucas Halliday, corporate wheeler-dealer, from the beginning. She'd never expected to have to apply it to a situation like this. "He does look exhausted," she said out loud, seeing him with Shirley's eyes.

"See what you can do."

He stirred, at that moment, just as Reba and Shirley arrived back at Maggie's little world.

Reba froze, not wanting to disturb his rest, even such as it was.

But then he grunted, pressed his fingers into his face, dragged his eyes open and saw her. "What's the time?"

"Six-thirty."

"You didn't need to come in this early."

"You didn't need to stay all night."

"I wanted her to know I was here."

"In case the ductus reopened?"

"No, Dr. Charleson said it would have happened by now, if it was going to. That's one hurdle she's over." He said it the way he might have announced the completion of an agenda item at a business meeting.

"You should make up a chart," Reba said, "listing every possible complication of prematurity. Give her gold stars in each square, or teddy bear stickers, for every one she avoids."

He ignored the wobbly, accusing humor. "All her levels look good." He was really speaking to himself. "Can I grab her chart, Shirley?"

He flipped through it like a seasoned accountant flipping through a budget spreadsheet, and muttered about various figures. Watching him with Shirley's words still hovering in her head, Reba saw the way his hand shook slightly, saw the fatigue-reddened whites of his eyes, and felt a stab of shock.

Exhausted?

No.

He looked *beyond* exhausted, as if he was subsisting purely on nerves. What would happen if he had a complete collapse? If he got seriously sick?

Instinctively, she put a hand on his shoulder and realized he'd even lost weight and muscle tone in the two weeks since Maggie's birth. He hadn't worked out in the hotel gym, or used the pool he'd told her about. He hadn't said a word about Halliday Corporation business, normally so high in his priorities. And, truthfully, neither of them was eating right.

Her anger evaporated.

"Lucas?"

"Yep? Want to sit down?"

"I'm fine. Stay."

"No, I could do with a stretch." His limbs practically creaked as he stood up.

"Let's…" What? She'd forgotten. What did people do when they needed a break? Normal people. People who didn't have their newborn baby in the NICU, weighing less than two pounds, still hugely at risk. "Uh, let's go for breakfast somewhere in a little while," she suggested, not taking the chair he offered.

Did he realize that he was swaying?

She almost reached out her arms to catch him and sit him down again, but he steadied and worked his arms over his head, loosening his long spine.

"You mean not at the hospital?" He frowned.

"There are these places called restaurants. You'd be amazed. They have these big menus, and the staff come to you to find out what you want. You don't have to line up and point. The scrambled eggs are made fresh, not left sitting for an hour in a metal dish over a big tray of hot water."

"Comedian, this morning."

"Pretty shaky at it."

"Still…"

"Hungry, Lucas. And a bit desperate. Remind me what color the sky is, again?"

"Yellow, last time I looked."

"Blotchy yellow? Because you were so tired. You were probably about to faint. We both need to get out of here. Shirley, um, pointed it out. When it's daylight. And not so we can just crash over cold cereal in our hotel suite."

He looked at her in silence, his gaze flicking up and down, catching on a couple of details, here and there. She was wearing yesterday's shirt and, yes, okay, it had a dried drop or two of last night's pasta sauce spilled on it because the fork had felt so heavy in her hand she hadn't held it straight. She needed to get laundry done…

"Okay," he said eventually. "But only after Dr. Charleson's stopped by. He said last night he would, before he went off call this morning."

"How are those two doing?" Angela asked Shirley, during their shift change-over conference, beside Maggie's isolette.

The two nurses both looked over at Reba and Lucas, who stood out of earshot at the water cooler near the nurses' station. Then they looked back at Maggie.

The tiny baby was still receiving one-on-one care, and would be until she outgrew the likelihood of some of the common preemie problems that were still a very real concern. Staff never dwelled on those, to parents, but they didn't hide them, either. Baby Maggie wasn't out of the woods yet, and neither were her parents.

"Wearing themselves out," Shirley answered. "Don't you just ache for the ones who care this much?"

"Oh, truly! And I'm not sure what to think with these two. They're not married, right?"

"No, apparently not, but that doesn't necessarily mean very much."

"So you think they have a strong commitment?" Angela asked.

"To Maggie, totally. To each other?"

"That's what I meant."

Shirley sighed. "I'm not going to go there. I'd just like to see both of them take a little more time away from here. Otherwise I'm not taking bets on which of them is going to collapse soonest, and in the most spectacular fashion. I told Reba she needed to get Lucas to take some time, but really it was just as much for her sake."

"So I'll tell him the same thing. If they're prepared to do it for each other, that says something about how they feel, don't you think?"

"You're such a romantic, Angela!"

Angela shrugged. "Is it wrong to want a happy ending, and two loving parents for this little girl?"

"It's not wrong. Doesn't mean it's going to happen. Let's just focus on getting her strong, and getting her parents to take some time for themselves. The rest, they have to do on their own, if they can."

Dr. Charleson didn't get to Maggie for another hour, but when he did, the news remained good. He took the stethoscope from his ears and told them, "Her heart sounds beautiful, now, just the way it should, and that's confirmed by all her figures. Her gut is good. We've turned the settings on her respirator a little lower, and she's doing the extra work herself."

"Oh, that's so good!" Reba breathed. "That's so great!"

She laughed and her eyes went bright with tears. She clasped her hands together, then flattened them against her chest, just above her breasts, and the laughter dropped away. With closed eyes, she muttered something about wrestling with the beast, which Lucas was too tired and unfocused to understand at first.

He was worried about Reba, this morning. There was something about her restless energy that he didn't like. He'd been sending her back to their suite every night and she hadn't argued, but that didn't mean she was resting the way she should.

And she'd begun to develop quite a tearful, combative relationship with the electric breast milk pump. She swore at it, sometimes. The words she used were mild, but the tone was anything but. She probably spoke like that to stubborn yearling cattle at shipping time, while herding them out of a corral.

It didn't fit the peaceful, madonnalike image portrayed on the cover of the breast pump's instruction booklet, but it certainly fit the effort she had to put in to get results— precious drops of the perfect nutrition for Maggie.

Okay, now he understood. Of course. This was the "beast" she'd just talked about. She needed to go and pump. He could see her switching from her happiness at the news about Maggie to a combination of determination and reluctance that twisted his heart.

"Fun, fun, fun!" she said.

Hell, he should have been more on top of this—on top of Reba's energy levels. He should have been the one teasing her about the existence of restaurants, not the other way around. He didn't normally let half his obligations slip, like that.

Yes, they should definitely go out for breakfast, as soon as she was done, and then some retail therapy at a really good mall. He'd never met a woman, yet, who wouldn't consider that the perfect cure for practically anything.

He asked Angela, who directed him to a place called Cherry Creek, where he and Reba found a quiet little restaurant and shared a fruit platter, as well as each ordering juice, eggs, bacon, coffee and toast—all of it fresh and delicious compared to the indifferent hospital food.

By the time they'd finished, all of the mall's stores were open. Acres of marble and granite gleamed, plate glass display windows reflected the ambient lighting without a fingermark in sight, and he told Reba, "I have credit cards burning a hole in my wallet. What shall we buy for Maggie?"

They browsed a store full of plush toys and chose a squishy, rainbow-colored soccer ball and a little pink and white bear. Wandering farther, they found an elegant children's clothing store, full of top quality American and European-made outfits that even a hardened financier such as himself couldn't help but consider adorable. Delicately stitched pastel playsuits and dresses, miniature fabric shoes, stretchy nightwear featuring ladybugs and buttercups.

"The sizes are all so huge," Reba said. "There's nothing small enough for her."

"She'll grow. How about this little dress with the overskirt? Or this playsuit with the embroidery? And the white shoes? I know, they're as big as boats, but one day they'll fit."

Reba lifted the smallest size coral pink dress off the rack and held it up. The gauzy overskirt looked misty in the store's clear white light. She riffled her hand along the row of lilac and lemon playsuits. And then she fisted her hands into the delicate fabric of the pink dress and scrunched it into messy creases without even knowing what she was doing.

"I can't," she said.

"If these are too fancy for a little cowgirl, we can try a different store."

"No. I just can't." Her voice was panicky and tight. "Not today. Not…not yet."

She stood in front of the dress rack with her eyes closed and her head bowed, and now Lucas understood what she meant. Understood, too, that she didn't even dare to put her superstition into words.

She couldn't buy these miniature-yet-still-too-big clothes for Maggie, in case Maggie never—in case she didn't get a chance to—

"Let's get out of here," he said. "Let's just go. Now."

He hooked the creased dress back on the rack, took Reba's hand in his and pulled her out of the store with his jaw aching so hard it felt as if it might crack.

The sales clerk's cheery, "Have a great day!" seemed to chase after them like a malign spirit, and he felt a powerful, primitive urge to wheel around and yell at her about just what kind of great days he and Reba had been having for the past two weeks, how many more such days there might be, and how did *anyone* have the gall and the insensitivity to say something like that to people who could be grieving, terrified, in pain…

He took a deep breath and coached the rage away, with a painful effort at staying rational.

It wasn't the sales clerk's fault. She didn't know. How could she?

And, hell, maybe it was the best thing she could have said. He and Reba needed a great day.

Desperately.

"I'm sorry, Lucas." Reba's tone was foggy, the sound of her voice barely louder than a whisper.

"It's okay. I understand." He still had her hand locked in his, and it probably hurt, the way he was gripping. Again, he had to coach himself, with the small part of his rational brain that still functioned, to soften his fingers, lace them through hers, turn the contact into a caress instead of a clamp.

"We should get back to the hospital," she said.

Yeah, to the fluorescent lighting, the institutional food, breathing alarms going off, other parents in tears, doctors too busy to talk. All of that would definitely make it into a great day!

"No," he told her. "Not yet. That's just going to plunge us right back into— Let's window shop for a while, or something. I…uh…couldn't help but notice you have a spot or two on your top."

"Pasta sauce." She tried to joke about it. "Latest designer accessory. I haven't managed to get laundry done."

Another thing he could have stayed on top of, on her behalf.

"So we'll buy you some new stuff," he answered. "What else? His 'n hers haircuts? Mine's driving me nuts."

He riffled a hand through a section that shouldn't be sticking crookedly up from the back of his head, the way it was. He hadn't brushed it since…couldn't remember. Day before yesterday, possibly.

"The place is quiet, this morning," he said. "We should be able to get walk-in appointments. There must be more than one salon here. Then we'll go back to the hotel and swim in that pool."

"I forgot to get Carla to pack me a swimsuit."

"So you'll buy a swimsuit, too."

"Maggie—"

"—wants you to have a new swimsuit."

"Oh, she does?"

Aha, he'd gotten her to laugh! Note to self—get printouts of humorous anecdotes off the Internet, tune the TV in the hotel suite to sit com rerun channels, call the executive handling his workload in New York and ask her to express mail some joke books.

"She's very fashion-conscious," he continued, as if this was easy, instead of a huge, painful effort. "It's, like, a total drag for her to have a Mom who wears three-minutes-ago swimsuits."

"I guess it would be." Reba was working at it as hard as he was, he could tell. "So what does she want me to get?"

"Something hot. Oops, no, that's me."

"You want me to get something hot?"

She slid a sideways look at him—a real, genuine sideways look, instead of a fake, effortful, trying-too-hard-to-be-funny one—right at the same moment when he was sliding the same sideways look at her, and the two looks met half way with a crash of sparks.

Yeah, that's right, I remember now, he thought.

Last September. The sizzle, the edge, the overpowering and almost competitive attraction they'd both almost forgotten, over the past two weeks, what with so much else overlaid on top.

"Yes," he told her, keeping the lock on their gaze. "I would very much like to see you in something hot, Rebecca Grant."

But they had haircuts first—Reba's was just a trim and a conditioning treatment—sitting side by side in the black vinyl chairs, pretending to read magazines while secretly sneaking glances at each other, via the wall of mirrors in front of them, to check if the other one was…well…still sneaking glances.

What was happening here?

The rational section of Lucas's severely compromised brain elbowed the out-of-control emotional section into a tighter space and said very clearly, "Careful! You thought this was just a fun interlude last year, and look what happened. You're connected to this woman, for good or ill, through Maggie. That means any other connection you make with her has to be thought through a lot harder. Don't blow it. Make sure you know what you really want."

Yeah, didn't he already know what he wanted?

Her body, back in his arms, twisting, responsive, giving, electric, hot.

Beyond that…

"My point exactly," said that really annoying rational brain lobe.

Beyond that, he had no idea, and not a lot of faith, and he couldn't pretend those issues weren't important. They were critical. For Maggie's sake, they couldn't afford to get to the point where they hated each other.

Stick with the retail therapy for now, big guy.

They shopped for a couple of hours, including a break for ice cream.

Lucas's idea.

Sitting across from Reba at their small table, he had to mistrust his motivation for suggesting it. Just to give them both more time out? Who was he kidding? Seriously, hadn't he just wanted to watch the way she opened her full, sensitive mouth? The way she narrowed her eyes in sensuous appreciation of the taste? The way she licked the sticky pink and cream scoops?

What had he told himself about wanting her so much, only an hour ago?

For the moment, he couldn't remember.

She bought two tops, a spring skirt, and a swimsuit that she refused to let him see until they got back to the hotel. She put it on in the bathroom, then emerged to perform a laughing and gawky-cum-graceful parody of a catwalk sashay.

And it was…strange, because the rational Halliday brain insisted, *This suit is not hot. There is not enough skin showing for that.* But other sections of the Halliday anatomy didn't take any notice of this assessment.

It was just a simple black two-piece, with a whole three inches of skin showing around the middle of her rapidly flattening belly, where he glimpsed a stretch mark or two. But it showed off her long legs and her long body, and clung to taut breasts that filled their cups to overflowing.

"Would Maggie approve?" she asked, pivoting.

"Maggie might not. She has teen fashion magazine taste. I'm not sure where we went wrong, there."

"Maybe we're letting her watch too much TV."

"I approve, however."

"I'll have to content myself with that, I guess."

"Yeah, I guess you will."

They swam for nearly an hour. The early April weather hadn't yet warmed up, but the outdoor pool was well-heated and had beautifully landscaped surroundings. It felt great to lie back and feel the sun on his face and the buoyancy of the water, and it felt even better to power up and down until he'd done sixty lengths, loosening his frame, making a small start at getting back some of the condition he'd lost lately.

But then, while he was still doing his laps, Reba needed to go pump again, and Lucas could tell it hadn't gone well, after he got back to their suite, because she'd taken a long time over it and came out of the bedroom with a tight look on her face and a tiny amount in the sterile jar.

"Don't sweat about it," he told her. "Your section of the neonatal unit freezer is practically full."

"What if it's not enough for her to put on the right amount of weight? What if my supply stops just when she gets to the point where she can feed on her own?"

"Hey…" He tried to hug her but she shook her head and wrapped her arms stiffly around the front of her body before they'd even touched.

She paced around their suite and zeroed in on the book he was reading about a California neonatal unit—a responsible, factual, heartrending, page-turning work by a highly regarded journalist. She picked it up, flicked it open at Lucas's bookmark, made a strangled, angry sound, then snapped it shut again and threw it half way across the room.

"How can you do this to yourself, Lucas? Reading all this stuff? All these worst-case scenarios that we might never have to know about."

"Knowledge is power, some people say."

"No, it's not!" she yelled. "It's just terror! Let's get back to her. I—I just need to see her and touch her again."

At the hospital, Reba's red-haired waitress friend Carla was waiting for them, just outside the unit, and Reba seemed to have calmed down a little by this time.

"Oh, it's so great to see you!" Carla said. "I've wanted to come down since she was born, but the kids have been sick, and I wasn't going to risk bringing an infection. The nurses wouldn't let me in without you here. You look great!"

"No, I don't. I'm a wreck." Reba gave her friend a tight, warm squeeze, but she seemed pretty tense, so Lucas stayed in the background after he'd been introduced, a little wary about how this visit would pan out.

He detected a surge of protective feeling in his gut that spooked him. What was that about? He had no place interfering in anything between Reba and her friend. Carla had known Reba a heck of a lot longer than he had.

How much did that count, in a situation like this? Which was more important? A shared history, or a shared terror about the future?

"She's so small!" Carla said to Reba, a few minutes later. She'd been through the correct hand-washing procedure, and wore a blue disposable gown and cap, both of which seemed to fit even worse on her compact yet sturdy frame than they fit on most people, and contrasted wildly with several escaping strands of her red hair. She looked a little pale and queasy, to Reba's eyes, as if she'd had to gear herself up to this visit the way people had to gear themselves up to a dental appointment for root canal.

"I can't imagine—I mean, I knew, but I didn't—I'm sorry, I—" she said, after she'd looked silently down at tiny Maggie for another few moments. "You know, my guys were both such bruisers! Over nine pounds!"

She gave an upside down smile, that was part empathy, part apology and part helpless pride, and Reba felt ill with an emotion that she knew was envy, but couldn't do anything about. She had to tense every muscle in her body not to show it.

Carla's boys were still small, aged nine months and almost three. She'd been through pregnancy and childbirth for the second time just last year, but both her experiences had been so different to Reba's. Those strong, healthy babies had been born in nearby Cheyenne and were sent home, already feeding vigorously, when they were less than twenty-four hours old.

What would it be like?

To hold your baby at birth?

To see her skin whole and pink, instead of stained with jaundice and bruising, and with huge areas of it covered in the tape that held all those lines and monitors in place?

To go home with her?

To feel happy and proud and hopeful, instead of terrified?

Reba couldn't even imagine.

After the births of both Carla's boys, she'd brought gifts, she'd held the babies and she'd cooed at the warm, darling little bundles, but she probably hadn't understood at all, back then, Carla's feelings of love and success, just as Carla seemed light years away from understanding the very different experience that Reba and Lucas were going through right now.

"We still think she's beautiful," she managed to say. "Perfect."

"Oh, honey, she is. I didn't mean that."

"We wouldn't change one thing about her, except to make her as healthy and strong as she can be."

"Oh, of course."

"And her heart condition has resolved. She's put on some weight."

"Has she?" Carla's jaw dropped, despite her clear effort to keep her expression under control. "Wow, you mean she was—?"

"Even smaller. Yes. Redder and thinner, with more hair on her body, and her eyes only just escaped being fused shut. Not to mention the bruises she developed, from all the needle sticks. She still has some of those." Deliberately,

Reba didn't mince her words. "And the jaundice. For a couple of days, she looked as if someone had dyed her with mustard."

"Oh, Reba!" Carla whispered. Her eyes were bright with tears, but this couldn't soften Reba's raging, raw, rebellious heart. "I'm just, you know, in awe, that's all. About how brave she is, how brave you are."

"Brave? What's brave about it? We don't have a choice. And neither does she." Reba heard her own voice begin to harden and rise, beyond her control. Blood thudded in her ears. Her limbs were shaking and her queasiness threatened to rise in her stomach. "It's not courage, to be stuck in a situation you never, ever would have chosen and can't get out of."

Carla nodded tightly. "Right. I get it. Is she…? Is she…? I don't want to ask the wrong thing."

"You've done nothing but ask the wrong thing, and say the wrong things, ever since you walked in, Carla."

"Oh, Reba, I—"

"Don't, if it's so hard. I don't need to stand here and watch you gritting your teeth about this, comparing her with your boys."

"Oh, honey, I'm not. Not in a bad way."

"Oh, stop! Just leave. Okay?"

"I'm sorry," Carla whispered.

She put one hand to her mouth and one hand to her stomach and fled for the door, almost stumbling between two empty isolettes parked crookedly on either side of it. In another moment, she had disappeared, and so, very slowly, did the agonizing rage that had swelled inside Reba like poison.

Damn, damn, damn!

She wheeled around, close to tears herself, and found

Lucas watching her. He'd heard every word, although she'd been in such a fog of pain and wild hatred of the whole universe that she hadn't even thought about him. Now, his eyebrows were slightly raised, as were his shoulders, and his whole expression was wary.

"That went well," he said. "Nice when someone cares enough to come all this way."

Reba took several breaths that felt so painful it was as if someone was cutting her lungs to shreds. She bit the inside of her cheeks and the teary feeling temporarily went away, to leave an unnatural calm.

"Thanks for your support," she said.

"Don't mention it." Lucas clearly recognized at once that the calm was a facade.

They stared at each other for a moment, then Reba's whole body began to feel as if it was deflating like a balloon. "What did I just do?" she asked him.

"You exploded at your friend," he said, in a conversational tone.

"Did she deserve it?"

"No, not really. I guess she could have been a tad more sensitive, but it's pretty confronting, this place."

"I'd better go after her."

"You going to yell at her again?"

"Not this time. I hope. Maybe she'll yell at me."

"Want me to come along, as referee? Put you in a straitjacket, maybe."

She bit her lip and shook her head, recognizing that he had a right to say such things, after the way she'd lost control. "Better on my own. I really need to—"

Get my best friend back.

If I can.

Reba raced for the elevator, but the doors closed before

she reached it and the other elevators were all on distant floors. Still, she waited, dived into the first one that arrived, and pressed the first floor button with the jab of a finger. The elevator seemed to crawl down to the ground.

When it got there, and when the doors dawdled open, she raced toward the most likely parking lot, through the cold April air, but it was huge and she couldn't see Carla or the gray pickup she always drove.

Either Carla had already gone or she'd parked in the other lot on the far side of the main hospital building. Reba raced in that direction, cursing her lack of condition following the birth. Her lungs again felt as if they were being sliced into, and her eyes stung because…what if Carla couldn't forgive this?

She saw the pickup, finally, turning out of the lot and onto a side street, with a redhead at the wheel. "Carla! Wait! Carla!"

But the windows were up and Carla couldn't hear. The vehicle kept going, turned right at the first intersection and disappeared, with Reba still chasing it in vain, red-cheeked, breath heaving and eyes stinging.

Chapter Nine

"She lost it with her friend?" Angela said to Lucas, seconds after Reba left.

"Uh, yeah. Did you hear?"

"Some."

Angela was just about to go off shift, and had been at the nurses' station having a brief meeting with the incoming staff. Lucas had seen her return and hover nearby, at about the point where Reba started shaking and giving Carla her emotional definition of how courage wasn't the issue.

Reba hadn't yelled, because both she and Lucas instinctively kept their voices down here in the unit, as did all of the NICU staff and the other parents, but Angela wouldn't have needed to hear the exact words to work out what was happening.

"Should I have let her go?" Lucas asked her. "Do you think she'll only make it worse if she catches up to Carla?"

Angela flicked a glance into his face and didn't fully manage to mask her surprise.

Yeah, he thought, who'd have thought Lucas Halliday would ever be heard asking for advice? And not about stock options or pork belly futures from a specialist source, either.

"Most people don't take it personally," Angela told him. "If Reba's friend is worth keeping, she'll understand. I'm more concerned about Reba herself. How did the retail therapy work out today?"

"Good, for what it was worth." Already, their session at the mall seemed like days ago, although they'd only been there this morning.

"Wasn't enough?" the nurse suggested.

He sighed. "I'm not sure what would be enough, right now, Angela. A time machine? No, strike that," he added, as soon as he'd said it.

Weird, but no, he wouldn't want to jump ahead to Maggie's discharge, because then he would have missed everything in between, all those milestones he and Reba were both hanging out for—getting to hold Maggie in their arms for the first time, her first real feed, her growing back up to birth weight, her weaning to room air. And he wouldn't have been here for her, making those figures on her monitors improve with the firm cupping of his hand around her little body.

"No, there's nothing," he finished. "Nothing would be enough."

"Why don't the two of you get away, just for a couple of days? Maggie's doing real well, but she's going to be in here for a good while yet."

"Another couple of months, Dr. Charleson said."

"You know we love her to pieces. We'll take real good

care of her, and she should be ready for you to hold her
when you get back. Take some time while you can. Pace
yourselves a little."

"I'm fine," Lucas assured her automatically. "But Reba,
yes. It would be great if I could get her away."

"Home?"

"Wherever she wants to go."

An image flashed into his mind—the little mountain
cabin at Seven Mile. Dad and Raine had taken a look at it
during their brief visit to the ranch over Christmas, but despite all the firewood Lucas had had hauled up there, they
hadn't actually used it.

"What were you thinking, Lucas?" Raine had asked him,
chastising him with a mocking pout of her overfull mouth.

"I thought you'd think it was cute."

"You know that with me *cute* only goes so far. But I agree,
the setting of the whole ranch is spectacular. We're going to
put a little chalet on the cabin site, Swiss-style, and a real
home on that gorgeous site where that old place is now, over-
looking the mountains and the river, with an indoor pool."

Would it be a gift to Reba, to take her for a final visit to
the place where they'd conceived their child? Or would she
find it too hard?

He could only suggest it…then duck, in case she bit his
head off, the way she'd bitten Carla's.

She arrived back in the unit ten minutes later, breathless, swollen eyed and tight faced. "I couldn't catch up to
her. I saw her leaving the lot, but she didn't see me."

"She's going to understand, Reba."

"I have to tell her I'm sorry."

She grabbed for a wad of tissues from a nearby equipment cart and pressed them to her ravaged face. Lucas
wanted to soothe her reddened lids with his lips, and cra-

dle her tired head against his shoulder, but frankly didn't dare, right now.

"I have to hug her," Reba finished. "It's not going to be enough, just picking up the phone."

"Angela suggested we should head home to Biggins for a couple of nights, anyhow," he told her.

She frowned at this. "Leave Maggie?"

As soon as she'd looked down at their baby and spoken her name, she closed her eyes and pressed her hands to her breasts, and Lucas knew what that meant, by this time. They were filling and tingling, because she'd felt a surge of emotion about her child.

Eyes still shut, she slumped into the chair beside the iso-lette, not even needing to check its position because she knew the whole of this cramped space so well, including the exact layout of every machine.

"Time to play with the pump, I guess," she muttered. She looked utterly defeated.

He dropped to a hunch beside her and coaxed her hands away from her breasts, feeling how hot and tender she was there, even through her clothing.

"No…" she protested. "Lucas, I'm—"

"So you're going to leak, big deal." He brushed his fore-head against hers, feeling the soft warmth of skin and hair, then sat back a little. "It's purely a technical problem, and no-one around here will mind. We've seen it before. Look at me, Reba."

She did, quirking her mouth into an expression that said, "What now?"

"I think Angela's right. I think Maggie might need us to take a break more than she needs us with her, right now. She knows her nurses. They're as familiar to her as we are, and they talk to her and touch her and soothe her, the way we do. She's improving every day—Angela says we should be able to hold her next week—but you're killing yourself."

"You're the one who stays here every night."

"I'm not the one who's trying to make milk for her, with minimal help from the machine and Maggie not able to help you herself, the way a stronger baby would. And did you cry all the way back from the parking lot?"

"My eyes are an eight point three on the redness scale, right?"

"Eight point nine," he corrected.

"Wonderful!"

"You are wonderful," he answered her seriously. "You're doing a wonderful job as Maggie's mom. But let's do it. Let's take a break. In fact, I don't think I'm suggesting, here. I'm ordering."

She angled her jaw, with a glimmer in her fabulous eyes of the stubborn spirit he remembered from last September. "Oh, you are!"

"Angela's ordering. Maggie is. She wants to be able to snuggle up to you one day and have her meals the way nature intended. She wants lunch still to be there, not lost to your exhaustion and your battles with the pump."

Reba closed her eyes again and let out a slow, shaky sigh. "Made your point, Lucas."

"We're going?"

"We're going."

"Tomorrow. Two nights."

"In the afternoon. If she's doing okay. Back here after breakfast Monday morning."

"Deal," he said.

"Plan to put it in writing?"

"I trust you."

"Let me go pump."

* * *

For the next twenty-two hours, Lucas kept waiting for Reba to back out of the deal. A part of him would probably even have welcomed the excuse not to go. He wasn't exactly looking forward to leaving Maggie for two whole days, even in the competent hands of the staff he'd already come to think of as friends. He was only doing this for Reba, and for Maggie herself.

As they drove away from the hospital on Saturday afternoon, he felt dizzy as if gripped by vertigo. The world outside the NICU seemed vast, distorted, disorientating and unsafe. Without Maggie in his field of vision, nothing else seemed to make sense.

He admitted to Reba, "One tiny thing and I would have backed out of this. A half degree spike in her temp, a blip in her weight gain."

"Even a spell of distress," Reba agreed.

"But she looked good, didn't she?"

"She looked great."

"We have to enjoy this even if we hate every minute of it, okay?"

They both laughed.

Kind of.

Edgy laughter, tinged with doubt.

Lucas glanced across at Reba in the passenger seat of his car and wondered how someone could seem so familiar, and yet still so much of a stranger. They were both distanced from each other by their fog of exhaustion and fear.

He knew how she liked her coffee, and the shapes her mouth fell into when she ate. He knew the colors of the natural red-gold highlights in her dark hair. He knew how long she spent in the shower and how often she washed that hair and the lullabies that she remembered from her own child-hood and sang softly to Maggie.

He valued all of it, too, more than he'd ever known how to value such small, simple things about a person, before.

But he still had no clue about some of the really important stuff. How far would she adjust her life so he could stay involved with their baby? What ideas did she have about raising kids? How did she see her whole future, now?

And whenever that hot, astonishing connection sizzled back into life between them, as it had yesterday at the mall, what significance did she attach to it?

Basically, what did she *want?*

He sensed she probably didn't know half this stuff about herself yet, either.

How could she?

He'd had to walk her through her packing this morning, and run a last-minute bundle of laundry down to hotel housekeeping because she discovered some still-unwashed things that she vaguely insisted she needed. At the time they'd agreed on for their early lunch, he'd had to wake her up because she'd fallen asleep in the chair beside Maggie's isolette.

She hadn't asked if he had any kind of a plan for their visit, and that was good, because he didn't. He just kept thinking about the cabin, without even knowing if it would be practical for them to stay there. They'd probably end up in the same motel he'd used on his first visit last year. Or at her little rented house two streets back from the steak-house, if she wanted.

Right now, this drive north, at just after noon, felt like one of those escape scenes in movies where the car is screaming down the tunnel and the ball of fire is rolling after it, threatening to overtake.

Terrible comparison.

Illogical.

Maggie wasn't a ball of fire. Denver wasn't. The hospital wasn't.

"It's the emotion," he heard himself saying aloud. "You just want a vacation from the sheer intensity of the emotion."

He'd never experienced this before. He hadn't even known it was possible. Lord, what a sheltered, barren life he must have led!

He felt Reba looking at him, but she didn't say anything for some seconds, then suddenly she gave a gasp and muttered something under her breath. "You didn't forget the pump?" he asked at once. It was the only thing he could think of that might have caused her reaction.

"No. That's in the bag. The jars, and all. I—I just realized. First time I've thought. When I've pictured this—getting away—not sleeping at the hospital or in our suite—I've been thinking of the main house at Seven Mile." She shook her head, as if something had gotten loose and was rattling around in there. "What's wrong with me? That'll be full of ranch hands. I was seeing Mom and Dad's furniture, in my head. My mind's playing tricks."

"I've been thinking of Seven Mile, too."

"Same mistake?" In his peripheral vision, he saw her frown.

"No. The cabin. Just can't help thinking how fresh and peaceful it would be, up at the cabin."

"Oh, wouldn't it? Oh, it would be so good to be up there!"

"Cold, still."

"Snow drifts in the shady patches. But we could light the fire in the stove. We can check the forecast. The track will be muddy. Horses might be best. Saddlebags for our gear. We'd need to shop for food. And check that—"

"Hey, easy!"

She sounded quite feverish about it, mind ticking over too fast. Was her body healed enough for riding, yet, he wondered. Would they fit everything they needed in a few saddlebags? Would they use two bedrooms, as they did in their suite, or one? They'd only needed one of the cabin's bedrooms last year.

She wasn't thinking of that.

"You're right," she insisted. "The cabin. I want to do this."

And he couldn't talk her out of it, largely because he wanted to do it, too, and to hell with any awkward questions it raised about the unexplored and probably impossible state of their relationship.

"I'm so glad I found you home!" Reba said to Carla.

She was already fighting tears, she'd need to pump again soon, and she knew Carla would feel the way she was shaking, when they hugged. Would she stiffen and push away?

"Hey, what were your other choices?" Carla teased. "I'm here, I'm at the steakhouse or I'm at the grocery store buying diapers and baby glop in little jars. Stunningly predictable."

Reba pulled back a little. "You have to be mad at me, Carla."

"No, because I'm too busy being mad at myself. I did say all the wrong things."

"I was way too touchy about it."

"I was falling over myself not to—because I know, I *do* know, how hard it is, what you're going through—but somehow that only meant everything came out worse."

"No, I just took it in the worst way, even though I knew you didn't mean it."

"I'm sorry. I'm really a good friend, honest. Promise.

You just have to take it on trust, I guess, when I mess up like I did yesterday."

"I messed up worse."

"You had a better excuse."

"So who wins? Let's get this straight. Who gets the highest Bad Friend score?"

"Me!"

"No, me!"

They were both laughing now.

"Hey, are you coming in?" Carla said, squeezing her once more.

"I'd like to, but—"

"I can't believe you're here. I almost turned around again on the far side of Fort Collins yesterday, to go back and apologize, but I didn't want to leave Mom with the boys for too long. Then I kept wanting to call, but Chris said I had to see you face-to-face—he's all set to mind the boys tomorrow—sometimes husbands are great—I can't believe you're here!" she repeated, against a background of TV and toddler voices.

"We came up for a couple of days. The nursing staff kind of kicked us out and told us we had to."

"We? Lucas, too?" Carla peered out toward the driveway, but her view was blocked by a shrub.

"Yes, he's waiting, which is why I'd better not come in. I wouldn't let him get out of the car in case…you know…"

"What, I was going to greet you with water balloons or rotten tomatoes?"

"Something like that."

"Where are you staying?"

"We're going to try riding up to the cabin."

"Ouch!"

"I'm fine, now."

"There speaks a woman who didn't have stitches. Hang on, though. Both of you? That little cabin?"

"We really need something like that."

"Both of you," Carla repeated.

Reba closed her eyes. "No assumptions, Carla."

"I'm not assuming anything. I'm straight out asking."

"And I'm not answering, straight out or otherwise. Because I don't know."

"You must know how you feel."

"Yeah? Must I?" Reba squeezed out a crooked smile, then ticked off on her fingers. "I feel exhausted. Terrified. Sore-breasted. Dizzy with missing Maggie already."

"Oh, of course…"

"I'm itching to call the unit every five minutes that we're away, although we've promised each other we're not going to. I feel connected to Lucas, because I know he loves Maggie as much as I do and I…never expected that, to be honest. Not at all. A man like him. But we're so different. We're from such different worlds."

"Sometimes that doesn't matter."

"And we get angry at each other. Maggie ties us together, and what if we hate that, in the end? It's not enough. There are divorced couples all over the world proving that having a child together isn't the right glue for a relationship. How can I have a clue, right now?" She stopped. "Am I yelling at you again? I'm not."

"If you say so, honey." Carla laughed, and hugged her again.

"I'm really not."

"It's okay. Go enjoy your two days. Just keep it simple."

The advice made sense, but it was easier said than done. Reba no longer had a clue what "simple" was.

Back in the car, Lucas asked, "She's all right?"

"She's great. Me, I'm not sure I know how to communicate in the right way with anyone, at the moment."

He didn't contradict her.

They took a detour to Reba's little house, where she wrestled with the beast again, and produced her usual little jar to add to the portable cooler they'd brought. The place smelled fresh and clean, because Carla had been dropping by every few days just to check on things. One day, it might actually feel like home. Would that be good or bad?

Reba called her parents from her own phone, even though she knew Lucas would have to hear her. He no doubt disapproved, all over again, when she said, "Don't come yet. Just please don't. We still haven't been able to hold her. Wait until you can do that." But he didn't comment.

They called the NICU, also, and Maggie was doing fine.

Next, they drove to the store and bought the food they'd need for the next two nights—steak and pasta, milk and fruit, half a shopping cart full of different things. A blue sky overhead promised fresh, crisp air and a cold night. They'd definitely need the fire.

Matches, soap, towels…

In her head, Reba reeled off the items still in store at the cabin as they left Biggins and drove toward Seven Mile. Her parents had left the cabin pretty much as it was, during the move. The Hallidays had asked for this, apparently, and Mom and Dad had no need of any more furniture and household goods in Florida. This meant that the familiar quilts and linens, the crockery and silverware, the bookshelf filled with old paperbacks and the emergency canned goods in the closet under the stairs should all still be there.

She felt her heart lift, and some of her fears dropped

away. The mountains grew closer, cloaked in falls of snow that looked as blue as the ocean in every shadow. With the car window open, the cold air seemed to polish Reba's face until her cheeks glowed.

Then they wheeled into the front yard that she'd played in since before she could walk, and the house was gone.

Just gone.

In its place, lay a dark, ugly expanse of mud, rutted with the marks of big, heavy wheels and littered with the broken pieces of a terracotta planter box that Mom used to fill with pretty annuals every spring.

Reba was too shocked to speak, at first. A few seconds later, she was too angry not to. "You didn't *tell* me? You couldn't have prepared me?"

"Reba—"

"I wouldn't have come here. You set me up for this."

"Reba, I didn't—"

"Is it bulldozed? Totally destroyed? Or is it…? Where is it?"

Lucas had to yell to get through to her. "I don't know! Okay? If you'll listen for just one second! I didn't know Dad would have gotten this organized so early in the spring. Do you really think I *wouldn't* have told you? Come on! Credit me with some—I don't know just what you do credit me with, sometimes, Reba Grant. Not much, apparently. A few organizational skills. Which have let us down on this occasion, because it's obvious now that I should have called ahead to Lon. And no heart, at all."

He parked his elbows on the steering wheel, pressed his fingers together across the crooked bridge of his nose and blew out a frustrated breath.

Reba asked in a thin voice, "So what was the plan, last time you talked to your Dad?"

"Last time I talked to my Dad, we talked about Maggie. Seven Mile didn't even come up."

"And you didn't call ahead to Lon?" She opened the passenger door and climbed out.

He could follow if he wanted.

Or not.

"I told you, no."

Behind her, she heard his door, and then his footsteps on the soggy ground. She kept walking, impelled by sheer stubbornness to go and actually stand on that lake of mud where her family's kitchen and bedrooms and living room once had been.

"So you don't know where the house is?" she asked Lucas, not bothering to turn around. "If it still exists?"

A couple of hundred yards away, the corrals and barns and sheds still existed—incongruous in their grouping now that there was no house nearby. They could hear cows bawling and various mechanical sounds over there, as well as occasional voices.

"Dad was planning to move it," Lucas said. "He'd talked to a construction engineer. They had a couple of sites in mind."

She felt him beside her, as stiff and angry as she was, and turned to glare at him. "Would you care to share the location of those sites with me, at this point, so we can go look? See if we can find my house?"

"If you're suggesting I knew more than I told you, then yes, I did, a little."

He bent down, picked up a shard of the broken terracotta and threw it into the wind. His body moved jerkily, but the throw was still powerful and efficient, and the shard skittered into the winter deadened grass beyond the sea of mud. Only when it stopped moving did he turn back to her.

"But I wasn't keeping it from you, Reba, we just had too damn much other stuff to think about. More important stuff. Like Maggie. And I had no idea he'd move this fast."

Reba wanted to apologize, but she couldn't, because she was still angry, and it would have been empty, and not sincere.

"Don't you need to be fair about this, Reba?" Lucas said.

"Yes," she admitted. "But I can't."

"Is that an apology?"

"Best you're going to get. Thank the lord I didn't know about this, just now, when I called my parents!"

"Is this going to ruin a break that we need so bad it's killing us?"

"Well, let's see." She parked her hands on her hips. "Has the cabin been moved, too?"

She heard him swear, turned to look at him and found he'd gone white. "We need to find someone," he said. "Lon. Anyone. The damned house, for a start."

"You mean it's possible?"

Lucas spoke slowly, hating what he had to tell her, appalled at his own sense of potential loss. "Dad and Raine have talked about putting something else on that site, yes."

He didn't want it to happen, let alone for it already to have happened, any more than Reba did. He hated that he had a delegated responsibility for this place, but no right to make major decisions because it was essentially a playground for his father and Raine.

"Such as what, exactly?" Reba asked.

"A Swiss-style chalet."

She gave a stricken little cry, and started running for the calving barn. Lucas followed her, not letting himself sprint the way he wanted to. She'd definitely get there first, and that was best. He didn't want to get in her way, right now.

As he got closer, he could hear sounds that suggested the place was being cleaned—the rush of a hose, the scrape of shovels on cement, men shouting complaints to each other, the sound of a truck engine starting up. By the time he pushed against the big door still easing its last few inches shut in Reba's wake, she'd found Lon and she was frowning up at his face.

"Have they set it up nice for you?" Lucas heard her ask. "Do you like the new site?"

Only Reba! he thought. One minute she's so angry and hurt about her old home, she looks as if she's going to fly into a thousand pieces. The next, she's thinking about people she has no responsibility for any more, and making sure they're happy.

Pretty incredible woman.

"Sure, it's fine," the foreman answered her. "Views aren't so good—more cows, less mountain. But the plumbing works, and the heat, and the stove is level."

"And the cabin?"

"Haven't been up there. Too busy, with calving."

"But it's still there? It hasn't been—?"

"Not yet. You taking a vacation up there?" He glanced at Lucas, nodded and lifted his hand. "Mr. Halliday," he said, and looked as if he was about to veer in this direction, paying due deference to his new boss's son.

Lucas deflected the man's attention back to Reba, with a quick shake of his head.

"Hoping to," Reba answered Lon. "Just a couple of nights."

"How's your little girl?" Lon's glance again took in Lucas, and Lucas could see him mentally joining the dots: so this had to be the father of Reba's child? Made sense of a few things.

"She's little!" Reba answered. "Getting bigger. Slowly."

"Incredible what they can do for 'em, now."

"Yes. We're hopeful. We might get to hold her, next week. Her nursing staff are kind of making us take a break for a bit, though."

"Cabin should be nice. Plenty of firewood, still. Hallidays didn't use it over the winter, after all."

She asked him how calving had gone, and got a laconic report. Couple of stubborn ones still waiting to drop, corralled out back. Only lost a few. She looked as if she had about fifty more questions crowding into her mouth, but then she took a deep breath, clearly fighting to remember that Seven Mile's ranching activities weren't her business, any more.

"Well," she said. "We'll saddle a couple of horses and start our vacation, Lon, leave you to it."

"Good to see you, Reba. They're missing you over at the Longhorn. And Gordie is…" Another quick, somewhat uncomfortable look at Lucas, during which Lon drastically rethought his planned statement. He finished with a vague, "Yeah."

Outside the calving barn, Lucas asked, "Did you want to go look at the house?"

Reba shook her head, her face still tight. "There's no need. It belongs to the ranch hands, now, and they're happy." She cracked her mouth into a smile she was determined to get serious about. "Do you want to bring the pickup over, so we can shift our gear? I'll start on the horses."

"Sounds like a plan."

"I can say sorry now, if you want." She tucked in the corner of her mouth and spread her hands, mocking herself.

"Don't. It's okay."

They reached the cabin at around four-thirty, and it looked so exactly the same as it always had that the sharp, dragging ache in Reba's throat and chest eased at last. She peeled herself out of Moe's saddle, understanding Carla's earlier "Ouch!" on a more physical level, now. But the soreness soon faded and they'd had a nice ride, getting here. It had done her spirits good.

The air had begun to chill down already, and the cabin was in shade. "We'll need to get that fire going in the stove," she said.

"As a former Boy Scout, I'm offering," Lucas answered. "Unless you'd rather, while I bring in our gear and see to the horses."

Without saying much more, they both worked steadily for the next hour, splitting the various tasks instinctively, with no argument. Like the ride, it felt so good. Reba hadn't had the time or the emotional energy to miss this life over the winter, but, oh, she needed it, now! How would she ever do without it?

Just the feel of horsey leather in her hands, the smell of the smoke from the fire, the tang of spruce and fir needles mingled with the peaty mud and the almost metallic odor of the melting snow. The sound of water trickling, the snap of the burning wood, the glowing white-orange firescape showing through the glass front of the fan-forced stove, and her growing anticipation of a well-deserved meal.

"You pump, I'll cook," Lucas told her, as the light began to fade.

So she left her riding boots and socks by the back door, pulled a squishy old armchair close to the heat of the stove, nested herself in cushions, relaxed, closed her eyes and actually didn't hate the pump, actually got some impressive results.

Going into the kitchen to put the two jars in the freezer, she found Lucas presiding over sizzling steaks and onion. He'd already heated a can of thick vegetable soup, baked some chunky whole potatoes in the microwave, and tossed a tart oil and vinegar dressing into the salad mix they'd bought.

He looked at her jars. "Wow!"

"Am I the queen of this, or what?"

"You'd better be hungry now."

"You'd better have cooked enough!"

"Shall we eat by the fire? Want a beer? Shirley told me unofficially that it's supposed to be okay, at this point to have one, if you want."

"Yes, to both."

It felt like the best and happiest meal she'd ever had.

Lucas dragged a second armchair nearer to the stove, as well as the old, squat-legged coffee table that looked like some bizarre breed of dog, turned into dark wood. He put their beers there, as well as their soup in thick stone-ware mugs, sour cream for the potatoes and barbecue sauce for the meat.

Mom and Dad had left all their vinyl LPs and their old 1970s record player here, with its wobbly little device that could stack and play a whole five records in sequence. Lucas put together a medley of Hawaiian slack-string guitar, the sound track to the movie of *Guys and Dolls*, a 1960s greatest-hits collection, some Johnny Cash, and Simon and Garfunkel's "Bridge Over Troubled Water," and this oddly inspirational mishmash rolled along in the background as they ate, complete with needle static and the occasional warp-related jump.

They didn't talk much at first, just a few lazy comments about the fire, the ride, the weather and the meal, which tasted so simple and good.

By the time they'd finished eating, the room was so warm they both took off the sweaters they'd worn during the ride, and Reba couldn't help, um, staring, really, at the stretch of Lucas's muscles as he pulled the garment over his head, and then at the snug fit of his gray T-shirt across his chest.

"I remember..." her body began to say. "We've been here before, and we felt this way, then, too. We couldn't let it go, and we didn't want to."

He stretched, worked the muscles at the back of his neck with his fingers, picked up his beer, drained the last mouthful and looked at her across the top of the empty can, his thumb slipping back and forth over the surface of the metal.

Her body began to tingle. Wasn't his doing the same? Doing the male version? When he drew breath to speak, she expected some kind of seduction line, or at the very least an acknowledgment.

We're going to get ourselves in trouble again, aren't we?

What is it that gives us this connection?

Something like that. Which meant that his actual words threw her totally for a loop, especially since he spoke so slowly, as if he had to drag each one out, beyond a barrier of deep reluctance. "Have you thought yet about how you're going to manage, how you're going to structure your life, once Maggie comes home?"

No, she hadn't.

Didn't he understand that she was still too scared? He was looking at her so intently, with those liquid amber eyes, surely he had to see straight into her heart? She could see the tip of his tongue caught between his even white teeth, as if her answer was something important that he could hardly wait to hear.

She shook her head in answer, not wanting to say more. Not able to, actually.

"Had you, before she was born?" he said, pushing her harder. "Are you happy that you've stayed in the area?"

"Lucas—"

"I'm serious, Reba."

He shifted in the squishy armchair, leaning forward to rest one forearm on his knee, while he opened the squeaky stove door, added more wood and prodded it into position with a smoking stick. The glowing light reflected on his face, showing his fatigue—those little lines around his eyes, his papery skin. His mouth was firm and serious.

"Last year," he went on, "you talked about not wanting to lose your dreams before you even understood what they were."

"I remember, yes." During their drive down to Steamboat Springs.

"I always felt… I wondered how much of what happened between us was an exploration, for you, about what some of those dreams might be." He closed the stove door, sat back in his chair and looked at her again. "It sure wasn't something you did every day, that was obvious."

Defensively she drew her knees up to her chest and wrapped her arms around her legs, letting her bare feet rest on the edge of the armchair's seat. She lifted her chin. "How much do you charge for your therapy sessions, Dr. Halliday?"

"They're free, as long as I get answers I can believe."

"What right do you have to any answers at all?"

"I'm Maggie's father." He spoke quite gently, as if simply reminding her of something she already knew. And of course she did know it, she just hadn't let herself face the full implications before. "I have a right to know where and in what circumstances you're planning to raise our child, don't I? More than you had any right to know in advance what had happened to your old house."

"You didn't have to add that last part."

"No, okay." Silence. "It's not my intention for this to get hostile, Reba. I just want to know where you're up to, before we—" He stopped. Their eyes met.

Make love? She nearly filled the words in for him.

"—decide if we're going to—"

Make love.

Just say it.

"—have to get lawyers on board, or something."

No! Shoot… I was thinking "make love" and you were thinking—

"Lawyers?" she almost shrieked. "This has been so nice, and now you're talking about lawyers?"

"Only because it's been so nice. If it had been horrible, lawyers would have been obvious and I wouldn't have needed to mention them."

She glared at him.

"Does talking about something like this have to make the evening less nice?" He shifted again, and the fabric of his gray T-shirt rippled and tightened all across the front of his body. "I'm asking as a friend. Imagine that I'm asking in an alternate universe where we never conceived Maggie at all."

Reba made a little sound of protest and let her head drop to the back of the chair. Her eyes stung.

"I know that's impossible," he said. "For both of us. But let's try. For one minute. Where would you be now? Living in town and working at the steakhouse?"

"No." That had always been an interim measure. For too long, because of Gordie, and Mom's illness and—

"Then where?"

"Somewhere working with horses. In a landscape where I can breathe." That was always what she'd loved about her life at Seven Mile.

"And how will you fit Maggie into all that? How will you fit her relationship with me?"

"And you're saying this can stay nice, when you ask questions like that?"

"They're questions you should be asking yourself."

She closed her eyes, shook her head. "Not yet."

He was silent and she waited for him to gather the words to push her even harder, but when he spoke, his tone had changed. "Same reason we couldn't buy clothes for her yesterday."

It wasn't a question, but she nodded an answer anyway.

Suddenly, the warm room no longer felt like a haven but like a prison. She jumped up, grabbed half their dirty dishes from the coffee table and took them into the kitchen, where the air was still cool and beads of condensation had formed on the inside of the windows. The mugs and plates made a satisfying clatter as she stacked them on the metal draining board beside the sink.

Going back for the rest, she met Lucas in the doorway, and this time he didn't cloud the issue with talk of lawyers and plans and the future. He just took her right in his arms, buried his face in the hair that had tumbled to her neck, and held her close.

Chapter Ten

Lucas's T-shirt was hot from the fire, and so was his face. The dry cotton fabric pressed against Reba's body like an iron, while his cheek burned on hers. She could smell steak and smoke and soap and beer.

For a long time, they barely moved. Reba didn't want to, because if she moved, she'd have to think about which way—even closer to him, or apart?—and she didn't want to think about anything. She just wanted to feel.

This.

Him.

His strength, his heat, his silent emotion.

Before she could go beyond these simple things, he began to kiss her. It didn't take much. Just a soft angling of his head brought his warm mouth against the corner of hers. Its imprint was soft, yet so intense and so strongly felt that she could have cried. The ragged breath she drew in was almost like a sob.

"Oh, Lucas. I don't want to talk. Or think. Don't make me do any of that."

"No. Sure. You're right. I can't." His voice sounded hazy, just a murmur of breath against her mouth, more kiss than words.

She kissed him back, meeting his mouth with hers as his lips parted, tasting him with eyes closed. The kiss was as endless as a royal feast, like a whole slice of time cut out and shifted into another world. His mouth belonged against hers, and she had no power to question it. She almost forgot that there could be more to lovemaking than this.

Why rush? Why look ahead?

Just this.

The tastes of beer and wood smoke and male skin, deep on her tongue. The sounds that vibrated far down in his strong chest. The solid feel of his arms, his muscle-wrapped torso, his hardness against her lower stomach, his legs meshed with hers. She slid her hands down his back and rediscovered that taut backside she'd held last year, and those firm creases at the top of each thigh.

"So good…" he muttered.

He pulled the already loose elastic band through the final inches of her ponytail, releasing the scent of her shampoo into the air around them. Her spine rippled with sensation as he spread his fingers and combed them through her free-flowing hair, then let them whisper against the tender, hidden skin at the back of her neck. He never stopped touching her mouth with his.

Her breathing went ragged and deep, pushing her breasts against him. She gasped, went dizzy, didn't even want to stay in control.

The explosive crack and hiss of a log of unseasoned wood inside the stove finally brought them back into this universe, enough for him to mutter, "I don't know why I told myself this wouldn't happen, if we came up here."

"You told yourself that?"

"Dumb, huh? We have too much to work out, Reba. You know that."

"Is that what you were trying to do before, by the fire, with those questions?"

"Tabling the issues. It was simple last year. I thought. We both thought."

"Yes."

"It's not, now."

"I do know that."

"We have to be clear on the connection. Is it just Maggie? Is it the attraction, too? If it's both, what else gets caught in the net?"

"Only one way to find out, isn't there?"

"No."

He pulled away more decisively and veered back toward the fire. He must have known she would follow. They stood side by side, stretching their hands toward the radiant heat that glowed through the glass. The hairs on his forearm grazed and tickled her skin and he laced his fingers through hers for a moment before letting her go again.

It was such a simple gesture of closeness that it almost made her cry. He could show so much tenderness, some-times—seemingly at odds with so much else about him.

"Talk to me, Lucas," she said.

He picked up the thread as if he'd only dropped it half a breath ago, and left it up to her to follow his meaning.

"You see, you operate like that, but I don't," he told her. "I've been watching you, learning about you. You have a current of emotion that carries you forward, and that's dangerous, because it washes you up somewhere before you've worked out if it's the place you want to be."

"And you?"

"I'm different."

"And better? More successful?"

"Yeah, I think so. No, not more successful, but less prone to damage. I'm risking less."

"So you want to work out how we feel about each other, before we feel it?"

He laughed. "Don't knock it."

"It's impossible!"

"It's necessary. For Maggie. She can't have this, Reba. She can't have two parents who jump into bed at the drop of a hat, when their approaches to life are poles apart. She can't have mess, and emotions blowing every which way, and a different decision about the future every week. I'm not going to do it!" He sounded angry now. Frustrated and impatient at the very least. He stepped back from the fire.

"Not going to do it?" Reba echoed. "Not sleep together?"

"That. And I'm not going to mess with Maggie's grounding."

"Last year, you asked me to marry you."

"That was wrong. It was my lawyer's idea, because I'd talked to him about wanting to secure certain—" He stopped.

"Rights? Controls?" she suggested. Her scalp prickled and tightened, and her throat began to close. "Is that all it's about for you? Rights and principles and controls and certainties. Listen, if I could have *any* kind of certainty, right now, it wouldn't be about what we feel for each other. I'll go with the wind on that. I'll risk. I'll ride the roller coaster. If I could have some certainty, it would be about Maggie. Only about Maggie."

"This *is* about Maggie."

"I don't think so, Lucas. I think it's about you. Something inside you that I don't fully understand, but I don't like. Table that issue. Add that to the agenda. See where it gets us."

"It proves my point, doesn't it?" he said.

She sighed. "Does it?"

"We don't understand each other well enough to know what's possible, and what we want."

"Okay. If that's what you think. I'm going to bed."

He didn't try to stop her.

Upstairs, she left the main bedroom to Lucas and chose the little room at the back, because it was the one she'd always used as a child. Earlier, she'd opened the window a few inches to air the house out, but now she closed it to a narrow crack and made the bed up with the wildflower-patterned sheet and comforter set that was folded at the foot of it. The metal stove flue jutting from one wall felt warm to the touch, and more heat wafted up the stairs, so the room soon seemed to surround her in cosy, welcoming air.

As she undressed, she heard the squeak of the stove door and the creak of floorboards downstairs, as Lucas took a couple more logs from the cane basket next to the hearth and fed them into the flames. If he built up enough heat before he went to bed himself, they should stay warm all night.

In bed, a few minutes later, in the dark, she heard more sounds from downstairs. Footsteps, water in the sink, the scrape of furniture legs on the floor. He was pushing back his armchair, or moving the coffee table or something.

And it was strange, because maybe all those sounds should remind her of the fact that he was down there and she was up here, and they'd just had one of their not-unheard-of *heated discussions* so she should be feeling miserable and hostile and stressed about the distance between them, yet instead she had a sense of peace.

They'd argued, but the world hadn't ended.

They'd argued, but it was about each other, not about Maggie, whom they both loved.

They'd lived in each other's pockets for two weeks, in the most emotional, stressful circumstances she could imagine, but they were still speaking to each other, still tender with each other at surprising moments and still trying to communicate something real.

And this bed was so soft and familiar, it still smelled like lavender, and the needle-clothed branches of the trees were soughing in the night breeze outside, and…mmm.

The next morning, the sun was shining again, reaching beckoning fingers of bright light around the sides of the pale curtains and into Lucas's room.

Last night, he had built up the fire, turned down the air intake, left the dishes soaking in the sink and followed Reba upstairs only about half an hour after her. He'd slept like the dead for nine hours.

Passing the slightly open door of her room on his way downstairs, he could tell she was still sleeping, which was good, because she needed it. She'd probably been woken at some point by her sore breasts, and sure enough, when he checked the freezer he discovered two more little jars.

Way to go, Maggie's mom!

The fire had sunk to a few sullen coals and the cabin felt cold. He coaxed them back into life with a couple of twists of old newspaper and some splinters of kindling, and soon had the blaze roaring again.

In the kitchen, he washed last night's dishes, put on

coffee and explored the pantry, where he found an un-opened packet of pancake mix and a plastic jug of maple syrup, still sealed. Easy. His stomach began to sing for its breakfast, and the smell of the coffee must have sneaked upstairs and awoken Reba, because she came down, dressed and smiling—

Yeah, really.

Smiling.

As if she didn't mind how much they'd argued last night, how long they'd kissed and how suddenly they'd stopped.

Just as he dropped the last of the pancake mix onto the griddle.

"I'll cut up some fruit," she said.

"You look good this morning."

"Feel it. I slept! I don't think I even dreamed."

"Truly. I'd almost forgotten how it felt. Must be the air."

"You look good, too. You have eyes instead of creases."

He almost said, "So we're not mad at each other?" But why risk ruining a perfectly beautiful day?

After breakfast, eaten in front of the fire, they went riding, and the horses acted as if they'd slept well in their outdoor shelter after a hearty meal, also. Reba took him via a different forest track down to a bend in the river farther upstream from where he'd fished last fall. On the higher slopes, they were tracking through mushy spring snow in places, but down on the stream bank it had all disappeared.

"We'll follow this trail for a bit," she said. "There's a place we can cross farther up. Then we can ride the property line all the way out to the back road, if we want—we'll see the place where the house has been moved to, which I think…I guess…might be a good idea—before we turn back and come up the main track."

"Sounds good."

Most of the way, they could ride side by side and could easily have talked. Didn't seem necessary, somehow. As she'd suggested, they crossed the river and rode the fence. There was a broken top wire at one point, and she said carefully, "Might want to mention that to Lon," because this was a Halliday holding, now, not her family place.

They reached the back road, and she suggested turning back, but then on the section of neighboring fence that fronted the verge, she saw a couple of rectangular boards wired in place that interested her. Lucas didn't know why, and she didn't explain, just kicked her horse to a canter and rode ahead.

He let her, content to ride slow and lazy in the saddle and watch her firm seat on the horse, her straight shoulders, her flying hair. At the corner post that marked the intersection of Seven Mile, the road, and the adjacent property, she halted, dismounted and tied Moe to the fence before scrambling through it. The boards were blank on the back so she had to get to the road and look from that angle in order to read them.

"For sale," she shouted back to him, standing motionless in front of the board. "Gordie McConnell's ranch is for sale."

"That's a surprise, I take it," he said a few minutes later, when she'd climbed through the fence and into the saddle again, and they'd begun the homeward ride.

"Totally," she answered, then lifted her hand to point to a place in the distance. "There. Look. The house. Huh. Huh."

She waited for a moment, as if not knowing, herself, yet, what emotion would come bubbling forth about it. Lucas looked where she'd pointed and saw the familiar farmhouse-red shape. Behind it, on the far side of a low hill, he could just see the rooftops of the sheds and barns.

Finally, Reba sighed and shrugged and said, "Yes, if

Gordie's really selling the ranch—he must be, he wouldn't have signs up all along the fence like that if he wasn't—it's a big surprise to me. I had no idea. I thought he was set for life. I thought he might even eventually raise the capital to make your father an offer on Seven Mile."

"You speak as if you're angry with him, when you talk about him."

"I wasn't, when we first broke up. I've gotten angrier."

"Not supposed to work that way. Time heals."

"Not if someone keeps picking at the wound. There's no wound," she corrected herself quickly. "Gordie's had no dignity about it, that's all. He gets in my face, whining about us making a big mistake. I can't respect that. The wishywashyness of it. If we'd gotten married, he would have spent the rest of our lives giving with one hand and taking away with the other. I'm angry with myself, because it took me so long to see it."

"Let it go."

"Mostly I have."

"Except when you see his for sale signs."

"Something like that." She shook her head. "He couldn't possibly be doing it because of me."

She frowned, kicked her horse on again, and Lucas followed, curious, too. It came to him in a flash of insight that if a man ever did sell a ranch because of a woman, Reba was that kind of woman—the kind whom, for better or for worse, you never forgot.

Back at the cabin, they saw to the horses then made grilled BLT sandwiches for lunch. Reba filled a couple more jars, and Lucas told her, "Have a nap now, okay? Don't lose your momentum."

"My sleep momentum?"

"Sleeping, pumping. Just look after yourself."

"I'm not arguing, notice! But how about you? You're going to sit in a rocking chair on the porch and work on your embroidery?"

"I'm going to saddle Ruby and ride down to the sheds, talk to Lon for a bit, make a couple of calls."

"The NICU being one of them."

"The first." They'd left Carla's phone number and the main ranch phone number as emergency contacts, but there was no land line or cell phone range up here at the cabin. "As long as you're okay here on your own, that is."

"I'm fine."

Safe. Content. Untroubled.

Because it was the closest thing she had to home, he knew.

Until the cute little Swiss chalet took its place.

No.

He couldn't let that happen to her, if he had any chance at all of stopping it.

It was crazy, because he'd never experienced that yearning sense of home before, and in some ways he knew he wouldn't want to. If you had a place in your life that felt like home, then you could lose it, and you suffered what Reba was suffering now. If you had no home to begin with, you were safe. It worked the same with relationships. If you tested all the boundaries and the possibilities and the pitfalls before you fell in love, you had a hedge, a level of insurance, against the emotional risk.

His parents had never done that. His father, in particular, had moved blithely from one marriage to the next, in the belief that he wasn't creating any hurts that money couldn't salve. He was wrong about that.

"You have to look before you leap, Ruby," Lucas told the horse as he heaved her saddle into place. "There could be rocks, holes, snakes. You just have to."

So why have I let myself love Maggie the way I do, he wondered. I never looked once. And I parachuted. It's going to tear my heart out if…

Don't go there.

Problem was, he'd had no choice. Just as he'd told Reba last night, in relation to her own emotions, his almost instantaneous love for Maggie had washed him up in a place before he'd had the slightest chance to work out if it was where he wanted to be. He didn't want any other emotions to carry him along in the same way.

Last night, too, Reba had said there was something inside him that she "didn't fully understand but didn't like," and it had to be this—his business-oriented determination to have all the facts and as much control as he could before he took a risk.

Well, he wasn't going to apologize for that.

And he wasn't going to change.

Saving her cabin, on the other hand, could well turn out to be a different issue…

Lucas was back late. Not late enough that Reba was worried—after all, wouldn't he get back here faster, if something was wrong at the hospital?—but late enough that she had already looked at her watch and carefully settled on the time when she would start worrying, supposing he still hadn't shown up.

She heard Ruby's metal-shod hooves outside the cabin ten minutes ahead of her crazy deadline, and went to the door to greet him.

"Everything okay?"

"You mean Maggie? She's gained seven grams. She's fine."

"Who did you speak to?"

"Weekend staff. Helen, remember? She's good. I like her."

Reba nodded. "She wouldn't tell you Maggie was fine if it wasn't true."

"Took a bit longer than I thought down with Lon, though, and Ruby is tired."

"If you want to see to her, I have the fire going and I've started on dinner."

"Sounds good."

"Smells good, too, I can tell you."

"Hang on, I brought this up from the house." He reached into Ruby's saddle-bag and pulled out a bottle of red wine. "I thought it might go better with pasta than the beer."

"I'll hunt up a corkscrew."

Back in the kitchen, putting a foil-wrapped packet of garlic bread into the oven and a packet of cheese ravioli into a pot of boiling water, Reba wondered what exactly had kept Lucas so long, this afternoon. Problems with the ranch? Business phone calls to New York?

He'd been so focused on Maggie for the past two weeks, he must have let a lot of things slide. She'd expected him to make use of the business center at the hotel, but when he did, it was only to look up preemie-related topics on the Internet.

They'd both begun to surface a little since leaving Denver yesterday, to take notice of other things—like a hauled away house, and a neighboring ranch for sale. Tomorrow, back in the NICU, she suspected it would all quickly fade again.

Suppressing a powerful longing for Maggie, she forced herself to focus on the present moment, instead—on the crackling sound of the fire in the other room, on the rich red glow of the wine when she poured it into two glass tumblers, on the smell of garlic and mushrooms and cream sauce.

There was a danger in focusing on the present moment,

though, especially later, when her glass of wine had seeped into her veins and softened her limbs. The present moment contained too much Lucas.

Still wearing the pair of old riding boots he'd borrowed from the tack room at the ranch, he had his feet propped on the edge of the cane wood basket and his whole body stretched back in his chair, with his arms wrapped around his head. When she looked across at him, he saw it at once, and gave her a slow, lazy, gorgeous smile. "Nice meal. Now I'm falling asleep," he said.

"So am I."

"Want me to carry you upstairs?" He still had his gaze fixed on her face. The fire light was so soft and warm. His half-closed eyes looked black.

"As long as you promise to put me on the right bed," Reba answered, wishing she sounded firmer about it... wishing she *felt* firmer about it.

"Which one is that?"

"You know. The same one as last night. The little, skinny, dipped-in-the-middle, one-person-only bed."

The safe bed.

The lonely bed.

The bed where she'd probably think about him all night, even if he wasn't there.

"I promise." He stretched again, as if preparing to haul himself to his feet and actually do it, actually pick her up, slide his warm hands under her back and thighs, cradle her against his chest and carry her.

Reba told him quickly, "I wasn't serious."

"About which bed you want?"

"About you carrying me."

He laughed, then blew out a breath. "Good decision. Admirable clarity of insight."

Because they both knew that if he got hold of her, if she felt his arms around her and his shoulder against her cheek in reality, instead of only in imagination, they'd end up in his room, taking full advantage of the larger bed, despite all his clearheaded arguments against it.

"I'm going to take the plates into the kitchen and soak them in the sink overnight," Reba said carefully. "And then I'm going straight upstairs. Why don't you build up the fire for the night? By the time you've done that—"

"—you'll be safely out of my way. Again, impeccable decision-making, faultless strategy."

"Are we laughing about this?"

"We're trying to. We're wondering if the wine was the right idea, after all."

"I'm going, Lucas."

"I won't look."

She narrowed her eyes as if to say, huh?

"I've always liked your back view a little too much," he drawled, and she went hot all over.

Reba didn't fall asleep quite so quickly that night, but once she did, her rest was deep and she didn't awaken until first light, when her rock-hard breasts demanded action. Going downstairs, she built up the fire and sat in front of it, and by the time she'd put her jars in the freezer she was too awake and the light was too bright to think of sleeping again.

She went out and fed the horses then made a big farm breakfast, cooking a batch of hot biscuits inside the stove, in the old cast iron camp oven that had been here for as long as she could remember, crisping bacon on the griddle, and adding eggs when she heard Lucas coming down the stairs.

They didn't spend long over the meal, and began to pack up with impatient efficiency as soon as it was over.

Although Lucas didn't say so out loud, Reba knew he shared her own sense that today was like the last day of summer school vacation. You couldn't cling to it the way you wanted. Awareness of what was coming next impinged too strongly. They'd be back at the hospital in a few hours.

Suddenly she felt desperate to see Maggie again.

"All her stats still looked good when I took over from Helen," Shirley reported to Angela, at the Monday morning shift change, after a long night. "Although her heart monitor went off several times in the early evening, Helen said. Phil and Cynthia both took a look at her and decided to notch up her ventilator settings, just after I came on. But her color still wasn't looking too great, or her oxygen sats. And when I took her temp at midnight…"

She handed the chart over to Angela, who muttered, "Looks like she got sicker pretty fast after that. When are Reba and Lucas due back?"

"Sometime today. This morning, I think. By lunchtime, they said to me initially, and I don't see them delaying. Helen says Lucas called just after she came on yesterday afternoon, and she told him that everything was fine. Which it was, then. I hate that this happened while they weren't here."

"Oh, please!" Angela raised her hands. "They'll blame themselves."

"And us, probably, for making them go."

"They won't dare to leave her side for a second, now. So she's on…?"

Shirley listed the medications that they all hoped would combat the infection that had invaded Maggie's tiny system, and finished, "She'll beat this. She was doing so well. She has to beat this, Angela."

"I know. I'm not looking forward to breaking the news to her mom and dad."

"Is there a way we can call them?"

"Is there a point? We know they must be on their way here, anyhow."

"I'm going to call the contact numbers they left for us. I just think they'll want to hear about this as soon as possible."

"Let me know if you reach them. I need to take her temp and put up more fluid."

"Diaper, too." As always, the staff tried to group caring activities together as much as they could. "She's about due."

"Is Phil around?"

"Delivery suite. Baby Esposito is going home today, but looks like we may have another twenty-five weeker by the end of the morning. Mom's in second-stage labor right now."

At the nurses' station, Shirley couldn't get hold of either Lucas and Reba or Reba's friend. Cell phones were out of range. Land lines weren't picking up. It was still early—just on seven, but ranching people started their days before dawn and so did small town folks like Carla and her husband.

Shirley left a couple of messages, including one at Reba and Lucas's hotel here in Denver, but she didn't want to make them panic. She knew it was a pointless concern. They would panic, anyhow, as soon as they heard her voice. She spoke calmly but her words still came across a little stilted, on the different answer machines and message services.

There was just no way to spare them this news. At best, the infection wouldn't clear for several days. At worst...

Back at Maggie's bedside, she saw Angela reach in to change the tiny diaper. Maggie twitched and flinched and grimaced, not really awake but not peacefully asleep, either. She made little sucking motions with her mouth, trying to console herself, but she couldn't. As soon as Angela had finished the diaper change, she broke open a plastic packet containing a sterile preemie pacifier which she gently slid into Maggie's mouth.

"Go on, little girl," she murmured. "See if you can keep a hold of this."

But Maggie couldn't do that, either.

"Any luck with the phone call?" Angela asked, when Shirley had stepped back into her field of vision.

"I left messages," she answered, speaking low for Maggie's sake. "Don't know whether to hope they get them, or not."

Angela sighed. "You know what? I really hope they don't. I want to give them that extra couple of hours of peace before this hits them. I'm not going to try calling, since you've left messages already."

"See you tomorrow morning, then."

"With you handing me a happier baby, I hope."

"Want to drop in at Carla's?" Lucas asked Reba, as they rumbled over the last cattle guard on the road out of Seven Mile Ranch.

"No, I just want to get back. I don't even want to unpack our things at the hotel."

"We should have called in at the main house." He knew they probably would have, if it had still been on its old site, familiar to Reba, and closer to the ranch buildings where the hands were at work.

"We saw Lon," she said. If she'd avoided the house because she still couldn't quite handle seeing it up close, she didn't say so out loud. "He said there hadn't been any phone calls overnight."

"Yeah, but he'd left the house by six-thirty, along with

the other hands. I should have thought before that it would be a good idea to call. I've been focused just on seeing her. We'd only lose ten minutes if we looped back there now."

"Let's not. I just want to get to the hospital. It feels like we've been away too long."

"Want me to drive fast?"

"Drive safe. I just want to get safely back to her."

They didn't stop once on the journey, and every mile seemed to get harder.

"We shouldn't have done this. We shouldn't have gone," Reba said.

"It was the right thing," Lucas answered her.

It seemed clear to him, right now. He felt more relaxed. Stronger. Happier. More confident. Pleased with various wheels he'd set in motion regarding the ranch. Closer to Reba, too, and not just because he'd wanted her in his bed so badly, last night.

She would lose this panicky feeling as soon as they hit the NICU again, less than an hour from now, he predicted.

And he was confident they'd made the right choices, this weekend.

Chapter Eleven

"I don't get this," Lucas growled at Angela.

"These setbacks are hard, I know, because they're—"

He cut into the nurse's soothing speech. "Hard! As of around three o'clock yesterday afternoon, she was fine, and now, suddenly, she has this massive infection that you didn't see coming and that's already set her back—" he broke off, rustling her chart as he flipped a page, then continued "—to the point where she weighs less than she weighed when we left."

Hearing him with Maggie's sensitive ears, even though they were standing well away from her isolette, Reba wanted to tell him, "Don't talk so loud. Don't be so noisy with the chart. She'll start to crash if you do that."

She hardly cared about his words. What was the point of challenging Angela, or trying to work out *why* this had occurred! They'd been warned. Infections happened. Setbacks happened.

Yes, she burned with regret that she and Lucas hadn't been here, and she burned with regret that she'd kept her parents away out of some impossible, wrongheaded desire to spare them, but Maggie didn't need regret. If she could even feel such a negative emotion coming from the people who loved her—hopefully she couldn't—it wouldn't do her any good.

She just needed the love.

Angela's second attempt at a soothing response to Lucas sounded like white noise. Reba didn't even hear it. "Does this mean we won't be able to hold her today, after all?" she asked softly.

"Dr. Charleson doesn't think it's a good idea yet, honey," Angela said. "Maggie's battling with everything she has, right now."

"I can see it. Her color, the way she's holding herself."

It hurt just to look.

"She's showing signs that she's not tolerating any kind of touch too well at the moment, even the kind that was doing her so much good before. She starts to crash the moment we get near her."

"I know. I saw. Just now. Her oxygen saturation dropped."

"Tell me more about the infection," Lucas demanded. "Is it bacterial? Viral?"

"We're testing for bacterial, and there may be some of that, but we think the real problem is Candida. A yeast infection."

"Yeast?"

"Yeast is everywhere. We're full of it. The air is full of it. Our systems can handle it, but sometimes a preemie's can't."

"You can treat her for it, though, right? You are treating her."

"We're treating her."

"And it'll get better."

"We hope so."

"Hope? Just hope? You don't know?"

"We're really hopeful, Lucas, but—"

"You're not going to make promises," he muttered. "This could cascade into other problems. Haven't I heard this? I thought I wasn't going to have to hear it any more. Hell, look at her vent settings. Higher than they were when she was three days old!"

He blinked several times, squeezing his eyelids together tight and fast.

"I'm going to put my jars in the freezer," Reba said, so thinly that probably neither Angela nor Lucas heard.

As always, his insistence on details and facts and worst-case scenarios made her feel as if someone was slowing peeling the protective sheath away from every nerve in her body, and she just had to get away, escape, where she couldn't hear it and where she wouldn't think about all the vivid, unbearable pictures he conjured with his scalpel-sharp questions.

In the small room at one end of the NICU that was not quite a kitchen and not quite a medical lab, the refrigerator-freezer unit hummed. Reba had her own designated section inside it for the storage of her specially labeled jars. She opened it up and added the impressive set of sterile containers she'd accumulated over the past two days.

She'd planned to boast about them to the nurses.

See? I'm so totally on top of this now, I could give lectures. I look exactly like the picture on the cover of the instruction booklet.

Yeah? Who was she kidding! She was so tense her whole body had locked up, and she knew she'd be back to square one with the cursed pump.

And when would Maggie get to use all this, anyhow? Would she ever?

Standing in front of the open freezer, with its mist of frozen vapor rolling down her body, she had to fight with everything she had, in order to keep the faintest shred of hope.

Maggie needs me to hope.

She's strong.

She's fighting.

And her doctors and nurses are fighting for her.

I won't let her down.

"What did you do?" Lucas's angry voice hit her from the far side of the open freezer door. She hadn't heard him or seen him until he spoke. "What in heaven's name did you do to make Maggie come so early, and have to suffer all this?"

"Oh, dear God!" she whispered.

Her stomach caved in as if he'd punched her, but he hadn't finished yet. His eyes were like smouldering coals, red-rimmed and as narrow as slits. His jaw shook. Already, he seemed to have lost the light tan he'd gained out riding over the past two days, and to have stepped back inside the aura of rumpled, off-the-planet exhaustion and almost tangible stress that nine out of ten parents in the NICU wore, also. He hadn't shaved at the cabin and his jaw looked dark and rough.

"Why did you go into labor that night?" he demanded. "Did you get sick and not tell your doctor? Did you even ask him if you could keep working? When you started feeling something, why the hell didn't you say so *immediately* and take the rest of the shift off? There has to be a reason for this. A concrete—"

"Does there, Lucas? Why?"

"It didn't just happen, out of the blue. You could have spared her this torture, and us, if you'd just listened to your body, if you'd been more careful. What in hell did you do wrong?"

"Nothing." Reba stepped back, as if from a blast of furnace-strength heat. "I did nothing wrong."

She'd had to tell herself this so many times. Even after Angela's firm reassurance a couple of weeks ago, she'd still had black doubts, sitting beside Maggie's isolette at midnight or dawn. She'd asked Shirley, she'd asked Helen, they'd all told her the same thing. Not her fault. And she didn't need Lucas's accusations now.

He gripped the top of the open freezer door, then gave it a violent shove and it slammed shut, rattling all those precious jars—not just hers but the ones belonging to the other strung-out, exhausted mothers that both of them had met and talked to often by this time. He focused on the sound, clenched his teeth and sagged against the laminate surface of the adjacent bench.

He looked ill.

"Shoot, Lucas!" she said. "Do you think I haven't asked the staff about this? Do you really think I haven't thought about that myself? Do you think it didn't torture me all the way to the hospital, that night, thinking it was my fault?"

"Yeah?"

"Angela promised me it wasn't. Shirley and Helen promised. And I believed them, and I don't know how I'd have gotten this far if they hadn't said it. Maybe you should go ask the nurses yourself, before you break apart every moment of closeness we've had, every piece of meaning in the things we talked about on the weekend. Because I can't—I won't—I will not listen to you."

She fled the room blindly, left the unit, took the elevator and somehow ended up in the cafeteria just because it was a place she knew. The lunch rush hadn't yet ended and the place was crowded with people and voices and food smells. She stood just inside the entrance for several minutes, letting it all wash over her, not able to go any farther. Her legs wouldn't move.

One thought drummed in her head.

Her baby's father blamed her.

It hurt.

And it made her angry, which felt even worse.

A huge part of her wanted to tell him, "Fine, if this horrendous, unlivable situation is my fault, then let me be the one to live through it with Maggie. Just leave. No one's asking you to share the consequences."

But she slowly realized that she'd never say it.

Lucas loved Maggie.

He wouldn't be here if he didn't.

He wouldn't have made those wild accusations if he didn't.

And since he loved her, he had the right to be here, no matter how Reba felt about him, no matter if they couldn't manage to exchange a civil word. She had to cling to this understanding, force herself to remember it.

She joined the line snaking past the pile of plastic trays and the glass-fronted cabinets of hot and cold food, and mechanically took a bottle of juice and a carton of milk, looked at the sandwiches and the Pasta of the Day and just couldn't do it.

Maybe just some soup, for Maggie's sake. What was it today? Cream of broccoli? Okay, whatever. No bread roll, thanks.

Lucas found her when she'd already spooned half of it

down without tasting a drop, but she wasn't ready to listen to him yet, let alone forgive him. Maybe he wasn't here to apologize anyhow. She just looked at him, silently daring him to sit down.

He didn't take the dare, but spoke while standing. "I shouldn't have said it."

"Even though you meant it?"

"I should have asked the medical staff, like you did."

"Did you ask them just now?"

"Yes. I asked Dr. Charleson."

"And what did he say?"

"He said he'd just attended the birth of a twenty-five weeker who never even made it out of the delivery suite. Born to a drug-addict mother."

"You didn't think—"

"No, of course I didn't think you'd abused your body or our baby that way. But sometimes the mother does do the wrong thing. You didn't. He told me that. I'm sorry, Reba, this has been a hell of a day, and my emotions just got out of control. I shouldn't have accused you."

She tried to laugh. It sounded like someone sawing open a rusty tin can. "You spend half the weekend convincing me we need to be rational, we need to act in a logical, sensible way, we need to mistrust our feelings until we understand them, and then suddenly you attack me, and claim it's 'just your emotions getting out of control,' as if that's all that needs to be said. Is there a consistency, here, that I'm not seeing?"

"No. There's no consistency at all. I'm sorry. I don't know what's happening to me." He worked his face painfully, then rubbed his jaw between his thumb and forefinger, and she could hear his beard growth rasping.

"Welcome to the world!" she said.

He dragged a chair out from the table and sat down, and there seemed to be no words in either of them—or no breath and strength left to push them out.

Finally, after she'd finished her soup and her milk, he asked, "You going to drink that juice?"

"No. You have it. I want to get back to Maggie. And I want to find a phone and call my parents."

"To tell them what's happened?"

"To ask them to come, if they want to."

"Now? You wanted—"

"I was wrong. If I'd let them come before, they could have seen Maggie when she was doing comparatively well. Now, if this infection doesn't respond to—" She closed her eyes, shook her head, swallowed and tried again. "If I'm going to feel guilt and regret, it's going to be about that. Keeping my parents away. You were right. I shouldn't have tried to protect them. I shouldn't have tried to make a decision that was rightfully theirs, not mine."

He didn't acknowledge her back-handed apology, which was probably a good thing. In a situation like this, they could easily spend hours batting "I'm sorry" and "That's okay" back and forth at each other like hitting practise tennis balls over a net.

Instead, he asked, "How would you feel if I asked my mother to come, too? Not my dad. He's already told me he couldn't take it yet, and that's his decision, but I know Mom would like to come. She just didn't want to get in our way."

"Of course she should come, if she wants. I'd like to meet Maggie's other grandmother."

"I'll let her know. I'll call her as soon as I can. In the interim, let's talk about practical things."

It turned out he meant schedules.

Shifts.

Timetables.

Meal and shower breaks.

He didn't want to leave Maggie without a parent at her side for much longer than it took them to get through the equivalent of a nursing shift change-over conference, at their hotel suite.

"It, uh, wasn't very useful the way I lost control, just now," he said. "I'm going to blame it on low-energy levels. We need to factor in good breaks for both of us."

"Do we need to actually roster it?"

"Yes. We do. We need to keep tabs on our energy levels, the way Maggie's nurses keep tabs on her progress."

"We need charts?"

"I'm serious."

Yes, she could tell.

Serious and scared, and this was how he dealt with the fear—by trying to control things that couldn't be controlled. It didn't make any less sense than her own far more emotional way of reacting. It was different, but it came from the same place—what they felt and feared and wanted for Maggie.

"Okay, so what's the plan?" she asked, not arguing, keeping it simple.

For Maggie.

"Why don't I drive back to the hotel, try and nap, relax, get room service. You take a cab there at around eight or nine and I'll head back here to Maggie for the night, till around the same time tomorrow morning. We'll work it that way from now on."

"Twelve hours apart from Maggie, every day?"

"Twelve hours getting a break, knowing the other one is there, touching her if she wants to be touched, ready to call the hotel the second there's any significant change in how she's doing. Let's try it, Reba. We need some structure."

"You're the one who needs structure," she had to say.

"So do you. You might not want it, but wants and needs are two different things."

"You're heading off now, Reba?" asked Maggie's nurse—not one of her three primary carers, who were Shirley, Angela and Helen, but a woman called Lana, whom Reba hadn't met until this afternoon.

She seemed nice, but there was a reason why preemies were assigned the same small roster of staff whenever possible. The babies needed it, and so did the parents.

Reba hated leaving Maggie with someone new, when she was so sick. Would Lana read Maggie's signs right? Would she cluster the care routines as carefully as the others did, at a point where Maggie even seemed jarred and stressed by the soft sound of a single familiar voice?

"I don't want to go," Reba answered the nurse. "But I arranged with Lucas that I would."

"Then you should. She's been pretty stable the last couple of hours. Sleeping a little more comfortably."

"I guess she is."

But Maggie's temperature was still up a degree, despite medication, and when she had her eyes open they looked glassy while her limbs seemed limp. You didn't have to look very hard to see that she was a very sick baby, especially when you knew every hair on her head and every pore in her skin, the way Reba did.

In the seven hours since lunch, she'd barely left Maggie's side, and yet there was so little she could do. *Nothing.* Did the soundless, motionless communication of love count for anything whatsoever, when a little girl was lost amongst so much equipment, when she was feeling so bad and fighting so hard?

What would it be like to hold you, sweetheart?

Wouldn't it help you, to have you skin to skin against me, to hear my heart and my voice, and feel my warmth?

How can it be that you're too sick and too small, even for that?

But apparently Maggie was, so all Reba had done, the whole afternoon, was sit and worry and wait and look. She'd seen every grimace of discomfort, every dip or peak of the figures on Maggie's monitors, and she hadn't even felt all the aches building in her stiffly held body until she'd stood up to leave. Now they seemed to burn in every muscle and every joint.

"And you haven't eaten yet, right?" Lana asked.

"No," she managed to answer. "Or pumped."

"Go. We'll look after her."

That's what everyone said when Lucas and I went to the ranch. And when we got back...

What had he said this afternoon? That wants and needs were two different things? She wanted to stay with Maggie. Didn't Maggie need her, too?

It took a huge effort of will for her to whisper goodbye to her baby and leave.

As soon as Reba walked into their suite, Lucas could see she'd had a long, difficult afternoon.

She didn't even try to smile at him, just dumped her purse on the coffee table, sank back on the couch and launched into a shaky and barely coherent summary of everything she thought he would want to hear.

Maggie's state.

Maggie's monitors.

Maggie's nurse.

He cut her off before she'd finished. "I'll see her soon,

Reba. Don't track back through it all. It doesn't sound as if there's been much of a change."

"They're adding some new medication, but I can't remember what it's called. Uh! Or even what it's for."

"I'll hear about it when I go in. Let's get you taken care of, first."

He found the information folder containing the hotel's room service menu, opened it at the right page and went to lay it in her lap. She reached out for it and their fingers touched, and he couldn't help stroking the side of her hands with his thumbs, then sliding them higher until he reached the soft skin of her arms.

A tiny, weary smile quivered on her face, then snuffed out like a candle. "Thanks," she said. "Now, what is there in here that I can pretend I want?"

"I pretended pretty well with a burger and fries, earlier."

"Could I get those mashed, I wonder, to bypass the chewing stage?"

"Pasta? Risotto? You have to eat, Reba."

"Oh, I do?" she drawled. "Gosh! Nobody told me that."

He ordered her a chicken and mushroom risotto and a Caesar salad, and was told over the phone, "Minimum forty minutes." This would delay his getting back to Maggie, but he wasn't leaving until he'd seen Reba eat, because he strongly suspected she might not do it if he wasn't here to make her.

"Why don't you take a shower while you wait?" he suggested, restlessness surging in his body like pain.

He'd managed a couple of hours sleep this afternoon, but after he'd awoken the time had dragged. He'd ended up shooting e-mail after e-mail to Halliday corporate headquarters in New York, on trivial matters that various junior executives were handling quite competently in his absence.

And then he'd gone on the Internet and found some stuff on what could happen with preemies if they were kept purely on intravenous feeds for too long. He didn't plan on mentioning this to Reba, because he knew she wouldn't want to see it.

"You might feel better if you do," he finished. "Fresher. Hungrier, even."

But she just lay back against the couch and shook her head. Her dark, beautiful hair looked like the back end of a witch's broom. At some point, she'd lost or removed the circle of elastic that held her sketchy ponytail together, and he wondered how long since those silky, messed up strands had felt the touch of a brush.

He could see her brush, right now, its plastic tortoise-shell handle sticking up from a side pocket on her overnight bag, just inside the bedroom doorway. He went and got it, but came back to find Reba's eyes still shut and her face drained of everything but sheer fatigue. He sat down beside her, the brush in his hand, uncertain of his next move.

Lord, lack of certainty had been such a rare feeling for him in the past! Now it seemed to swamp him several times a day. Hating it, he decided to let it go, at least on the issue of brushing Reba's hair.

No more second-guessing.

Just do it.

He began to stroke the springy bristles through her wild mane—gently, in case he hurt her, slowly, to give her a chance to tell him to stop. She didn't, not with words or movement, so he kept going, soothed and nurtured by the action more than it could possibly be soothing and nurturing her, he suspected. Her hair tickled his fingers, and made a sound that reminded him of wind combing through the trees around the cabin at Seven Mile.

Her closed lids flickered, and she said, "Mmm."

"Lay your head in my lap," he whispered. "I can reach more of your hair, that way, and you don't have to do a thing."

Without waiting for her response, he coaxed her to topple toward him and nestled the back of her head across his thighs, propped higher by his feet wedged against the edge of the coffee table.

Her hair streamed out across the pale fabric of the couch. He bundled it in his fingers and swept the brush through it again and again, learning the shape of her head and the exact progression from fine skin to downy tendrils to thick strands at her temples and behind her ears.

He'd never touched a woman's hair like this before. He'd never shared the kind of emotional vulnerability with someone that made such an intimate action possible—the kind of vulnerability that made you want to tend each other's simplest, most timeless needs.

He felt a surging connection to this woman—this one, unique woman—which defied everything he'd told himself and her, over the past few days, about caution and good sense. With Maggie so sick, it felt wrong for her parents to deny the comfort they could take in each other.

Just wrong.

He couldn't hold back. Not today. He wanted to bury himself in Reba's heart and her body, and forget completely about the future.

Cradled in Lucas's lap, Reba felt the moment when his touch changed.

At first, his actions had been as simple and tender as those of Maggie's nurses when they adjusted her little knit cap or changed her position. Her whole spine had rippled with a tingling cascade of delicious sensation, and she'd felt so safe, suspended in a moment that had drifted out of time and simply stopped.

But now...

She heard the plastic bump of the brush on the end table beside the couch as he put it down, and he began to stroke her hair with his fingers instead. The ball of his thumb brushed across her lower lip. "I want you," it said, and her body answered in full agreement.

With her eyes still closed she lifted her jaw to try and find that tantalizing, bluntly expressive touch again, but she found his mouth instead. He gathered her up into his arms and she helped him, winding hers around his neck, parting her lips and printing her mouth on his, over and over, deeper and deeper, not wanting this to stop—wanting the whole universe to stop, maybe, but not this.

She remembered that they'd kissed this way before, last September, and again at the cabin on Saturday night. Two days ago. It seemed much longer. Time was so distorted since Maggie's birth, everything was out of place.

Everything except her mouth exploring his, giving him her soul to keep safe.

Her eyes streamed with the tears that still came so easily, and he must have tasted them, or felt the cool, stinging wetness. "Reba?"

"I'm fine. It doesn't matter if I cry. It's good."

"Is it, sweetheart?"

"Everything I feel is so close to the surface."

"Always. You don't know what that does to me. Makes me so hungry for you, takes me somewhere I've never been."

He muttered something she couldn't hear, and kissed her even more deeply, his hands moving on her body, stroking one taut, aching breast, curving around her hip, moving back and down to feel the swelling heat between her thighs.

She dragged her mouth away for a moment, opened her eyes and looked at him—at his steady amber eyes, his thick lashes, the new lines of stress around his mouth, poised so close to hers.

"Don't stop this," she said, her voice not steady.

"You think I could?"

"You have, before. Don't pull this out from under my feet again, now that we've gone so far. I can't remember any of your arguments from the other night, about why it was wrong. And I don't want to."

"Neither can I."

Maggie's infection had changed something in both of them. Life could be so frail. Connections could fray and rip for so many reasons. All they wanted to do was grab onto something good *now,* while it was here in their hands, here in their bodies and hearts.

When Lucas pulled her from the couch, she clung to him as if he might somehow evaporate or melt away. They reached the bedroom almost staggering, holding each other, so impatient. Reba crossed her arms, grabbed the hem of her china blue cotton knit sweater and pulled it over her head, then discovered Lucas watching her, riveted by the way her breasts moved.

Electrified by the evidence of his desire, she unhooked her bra, dropped it to the floor and let him see everything— the heavy fullness since Maggie's birth, the huge, darkened peaks of her nipples, the way her breathing had already quickened in anticipation.

"Finish," he said. "Let me watch."

She laughed, even though she still had tears on her cheeks. "It's that good?"

"It's better. Your hips. Your breasts. The shadow and the light. The way you move. Everything."

"Do I get to see, too?"

"You get anything you want."

"I just want you, no teasing. No delays."

She didn't even like saying the word. *Delay* reminded her of another word—*setback*—that had tortured both of them since they'd arrived back in Denver today. She just wanted to go forward.

As soon as he was naked, khaki chinos and cream polo shirt in a heap on the floor, he came and held her and she felt the prodding ridge of his arousal and the friction and pressure of her tight, jutting breasts against his chest. They rocked their hips together, slid across each other, ran their hands over whole landscapes of hot skin and tight muscle. They tasted each other, and whispered words that no one should dare to say to another human being, except when they were joined like this.

The bed covers were already turned down. He lay back and reached for her. She straddled him, feeling the weight of his hands cupping her cheeks. She trailed her lips across his chest, arched her spine to lift herself a little higher, so she could map his face with her fingers.

She found more new lines of stress, tiny ones, around his eyes. She kissed them, kissed every crease and every tightened plane on his face, wanting her lips to have the power to make them fade again.

Would their lovemaking do that?

It seemed possible, with such passionate sensation surging inside her.

Let my body heal you. Let my body make us both forget, just for a while.

He wanted the same thing, and believed in its power just

as she did. He'd even prepared for it, she found, when he opened the bedside drawer and tore one of the new foil packets littered inside.

"Let me into you, Reba," he whispered. "Let me feel you."

"Yes, oh yes."

Their need surged even higher, building like a storm-driven wave across the ocean, like thunder-heads in a summer sky. He drove faster and she clung harder, squeezing him, pulsing against him, flinging her head back and gasping as her climax splintered against his already convulsing body.

She clung to him for minutes, once they lay still, listening to the push and pull of his breathing, feeling it against her chest and her cheek. Neither of them spoke until they heard the rumble of a cart in the corridor outside.

"If that's room service…" Lucas growled.

They listened and waited, but the cart had moved on. Not for their room, apparently.

"It'll be here, soon, though," he said.

"You want me to bounce up and get dressed, ready to be hungry?"

"I want to see you eat before I leave."

"I'll eat. Lucas…?"

"Mmm?"

"What I said before, about pulling the rug out from under me on this—on our making love again—don't do it now, either, will you?"

"Like I said before, do you think I would? Could?"

"I think you might. I'm afraid you might. You know. Step back. Back-pedal. Go back on what we felt a few minutes ago, when it happened. And I so hate that word *back* right now." Her throat tightened. "I *hate* it."

He was silent for a stretched out moment, and she knew she didn't have to explain any further what she meant.

"Yeah," he said at last. "I hate it, too. You're right. Let's try not to go back. Even if going forward is monumentally doomed to—"

Rap-rap-rap at the door.

This time, they hadn't heard the cart.

"Just a second," Lucas called.

He rolled onto his feet like a ninja, making the sheets ripple and snap like flags in the wind. He wasn't going to let her nourishment escape back to the hotel kitchen untouched, he was going to hunt it down and set it in front of her and make sure she dealt with it as it deserved.

Reba knew they wouldn't get the right chance to finish this conversation tonight. Maybe not for days, or not ever. Did that matter? Hadn't they said everything that was really important? It wasn't too hard to come up with the general gist to the end of a sentence containing the words *monumentally doomed*.

She didn't need any further input from him.

She knew everything about what she'd given him, what she risked, and what she doubted he could ever give back.

Chapter Twelve

"Oh, Mom, Dad, it's so good to see you!"

Reba hugged her father, feeling his strong arms around her, then bent to hug her mother, too. Ground staff had met Mom's flight with electric-powered transport at the arrival gate because her walking wasn't so strong right now.

She didn't look as tired as Reba had feared, after the journey from Florida, but the gray roots of her hair were growing out behind the pretty light brown tint she liked to use, a sure sign that she hadn't been feeling good lately.

"How's Maggie?" she asked at once.

"Lucas is with her. Her temperature is down, and they think the infection is starting to respond to treatment. But she's still de-satting and crashing at the slightest thing. She's not out of the woods, yet. We can't hold her, or even—"

"Crashing? De-satting?"

"NICU-speak. I guess I managed not to use it when I

gave you all those updates on the phone. Her heart and her oxygen, I'm talking about. Oh, you wouldn't believe!" She tried to laugh, but it hurt her throat as usual. "We have a whole new vocabulary, now. We're incomprehensible to anyone in the outside world."

With Denver's airport so far out of town, their transit to the hotel seemed long, and Mom did look fatigued by the time they arrived and checked into a room one floor down from Lucas and Reba's suite. It was three in the afternoon, and Lucas was keeping Reba's regular vigil at the hospital.

"Maybe you should wait until tomorrow before you see her, Stella," Reba's father suggested.

But Mom wasn't having that.

"Just give me half an hour," she said firmly. "Maybe some hot tea. I'll be fine. I'm not coming all this way to wait another day before I see my granddaughter." She hugged Reba again. "I'm so glad we're here, sweetheart."

"I shouldn't have stopped you before. I— You know I just thought— But so much of what you think at a time like this is wrong. You don't think. You can't. You just— I'm so glad you're here, too."

At the hospital, Lucas peeled himself out of the chair beside Maggie's isolette, shook Dad's hand and clapped him on the upper arm, as if greeting a business colleague he'd always liked. "Joe," he said. "Nice to see you again."

They'd met a couple of times last fall, during the process of the Seven Mile sale.

Mom kissed Lucas's cheek, because he was her grandchild's father. "Are you taking enough time out? You look tired."

"That's all anyone ever seems to say to each other around here," Reba joked.

"And this is our little girl?"

"This is her."

"Sit down, Stella." Lucas angled the chair a little, and took Mom's elbow, his movements smooth, courteous and unfussed. "She's had a pretty good afternoon, considering." He reeled off the usual figures, and an amount of weight gain that nobody but parents of preemies would be crazy enough to celebrate.

Maggie was sleeping more peacefully than she had been able to for several days, but her little face looked so world-weary and old, and her skin was still almost transparent, betraying her less than optimal weight gain. She had to be exhausted by the effort of fighting the infection. Her immune system was too immature for a battle like this, even with all the weapons her staff had given her.

Last week, Dr. Charleson had been hopeful that she would have started to take some of her nutrition through a feed tube by now, which would help develop her digestion, but with her infection, he'd delayed this step, which meant that Reba's jars, so carefully labeled and dated and stored, still weren't being used. She had to fight her feelings about the pump almost every time she used it.

On the up side, if you really stretched the definition of *up*, no tube feeds yet meant one less piece of equipment taped to Maggie's body, one less piece of plastic tube, one less liquid to calibrate and keep track of, in tiny amounts.

She was still on one-to-one nursing care, and Helen kept her usual close eye on monitors and fluid flow rates, close by. Reba would introduce her to Mom and Dad in a minute.

"And we can't even touch her," Mom whispered.

"Not today," Reba said. "At least she can stand having us close. Two days ago, she couldn't even do that."

Two days.

Just two days since they'd gotten back from the ranch.

Lucas's mother was flying in tomorrow and staying for two weeks. Her visit would out-run Reba's parents' stay, because they were heading back to Florida next Thursday. A longer trip would tire Mom out too much.

Last night, Lucas's father had called with a gruff announcement that he'd be here not this coming Friday, but the Friday two weeks away. Just a flying visit, over the weekend. If that was okay, of course. Lucas had to be sure to tell him if it wasn't, and to update him if the situation changed.

"I got the impression the whole thing was Mom's idea," Lucas had reported to Reba, relaying the whole conversation almost word for word, just before he headed back to the hospital for his overnight vigil with Maggie. "Didn't think she still had the power to twist his arm like that. And I don't think it's any coincidence that he gets here the day after she leaves."

"They find it that difficult to deal with each other?"

"Unfortunately."

I'm so lucky, Reba realized now, as she looked at her parents looking at Maggie.

Mom sat in the chair, while Dad stood behind her, his silvered hair bleached by the NICU lights. He had his hand curved over her shoulder, and as Reba watched, her mother covered those worn rancher's knuckles with her own much softer palm, then their fingers tangled together and squeezed.

What would it be like to reach adulthood without having seen any evidence that love could last like this, even through hardship and tragedy and pain?

Maybe it wasn't surprising that Lucas put far more trust in facts and principles and structures and case studies than he put in emotions. And maybe it wouldn't be possible for him ever to change.

"Dr. Charleson's hoping tomorrow for the naso-gastric feeds to start," he said quietly to Reba's parents, pacing away from Maggie's isolette. The fabric of his shirt was creased and damp from the back of the uncomfortable chair, and the high heat setting used in a unit like this. "That's not within the ideal window, from the reading I've done, but it's still close."

And maybe it was crazy for the two of them to even try to connect, in bed or anywhere else, when they approached life in such different ways.

If Lucas hadn't been so strung out and scared about Maggie, Reba understood, he never would have let his control break down on Monday night. The two of them would still be keeping right out of each other's body space, flinching and fighting the chemistry every time they touched.

Did moms of preemies ever get their tear ducts back under control?

Her eyes were stinging and blurring again.

But for once she wasn't crying for Maggie.

She was crying for Maggie's dad, and for the fact that she felt so much love for him, right now, at a point where she'd just seen more clearly than ever—and she hadn't exactly been blind about it before this—how impossible it would be for them in the future to make their relationship work.

"You and Lucas don't get to spend a lot of time together," Reba's mother said, from beneath a thick swirl of wet, mousse-covered hair, "the way you've scheduled your hours with Maggie."

"If we don't work it that way, then we both stretch ourselves too thin, and ultimately that doesn't help her," Reba answered. "I wasn't sure about such a strict timetable, at first, but so far it's working."

"Was it Lucas's idea?"

"Ohh, yeah! It was Lucas's idea!" She smiled, to soften the statement.

But Mom pushed a little more. "That's what he's like? So rigid? He doesn't seem to be, in the interactions we've had. And his mother is a lovely woman, too."

"Yes, she is."

"I'd expected her to be harder to talk to."

"No, I wouldn't say Lucas was rigid," Reba answered slowly. "That's such a negative word." In a different tone, she added, "Okay, we're ready to rinse, now."

Mom leaned her head back against the towels Reba had used to pad the edge of the bathroom sink, while Reba opened the faucets and tested the water temperature against her wrist. She was helping Mom to dye her hair, before she and Dad flew back to Florida tomorrow.

They used to do this together at the ranch, and there was always something special about it. They would talk and laugh, or say some more serious things that weren't always so easy to communicate face to face. Busy hands and running water helped get down to that level, for some reason.

Reba filled a jug of water and poured it over Mom's hair, stroking it carefully back from her forehead so that the mousse didn't run in her eyes.

"No, Lucas isn't rigid," she repeated. "He's practical. He likes facts. He just wants to know where he stands."

"It's not always possible. Hasn't he discovered that, yet?"

"He's starting to. But he's still fighting it. And maybe he's right to. Sometimes, it helps to have guidelines. Mom, some of the things I feel about Maggie are so huge and unlivable, I might go crazy if Lucas didn't pull in the other direction, sometimes."

The water ran in the sink like music, softening the momentary silence between them.

"Do you love him, honey?" Mom said.

Well, yes, Reba should have been expecting that one.

In fact, she sort of had been expecting it.

This didn't mean she had an answer prepared.

"You're allowed to think about it, if you want," Mom offered generously.

"No…" You couldn't rehearse a conversation like this, you just had to open your mouth and see what came out. "I could love him," Reba continued slowly, "if I thought it would do either of us any good."

And didn't that sound like one of Lucas's own lines!

"It would do Maggie good," Mom said.

"Would it? If we didn't make the cut, after a while? Not everyone is as good at this as you and Dad. Not everyone is as *right* together. Wouldn't it be harder on her? If we pushed, and it was artificial, unworkable, and there was a horrible period of noncommunication and anger before we finally called it quits?"

"You think that'll happen?"

"We're so different."

Her mother thought for a moment, then asked on a drawl, "So does Lucas have a *timetable* worked out for when you are calling it quits?"

Reba had to laugh, even though it hurt. "He probably does. But he hasn't shared it with me."

"When Maggie goes home," Mom suggested.

Yes.

Of course.

It would happen then.

"Yes, because then he'll go back to New York."

As with most successful business conglomerates, when the Halliday Corporation acquired a new company, Halliday executives kept a closer eye on its operation during their initial period of ownership. Once they were confident that it was running smoothly and efficiently, they stepped back, and loosened their control.

When Maggie went home, her growing body running smoothly and efficiently, Lucas would let go in just the same way—not of his love, but of his need to watch every moment of her progress. He and Reba weren't just different, they came from different worlds.

And yet Maggie still linked them.

She linked all of them.

For Reba's parents' last night in Denver, everyone took a rare break from keeping watch over their little girl and went out to dinner. The restaurant they chose wasn't fancy, because fancy places were slow and Mom found it too tiring to sit up in a hard-backed chair for that long. It was just a quiet establishment not too far from the hotel, that served modern American cuisine.

"Dr. Charleson told us this morning that she's tolerated the tube feeds better than they thought she would, in the days since she started them, so they're going to increase those from tomorrow," Lucas announced, after the five of them had ordered. "Make them a higher percentage of her total calorie intake."

"That's wonderful news!" his mother Kate exclaimed, lifting her glass so that the moment turned into a toast to Maggie's health and future.

"Does he think the infection is fully resolved, then?" Reba's father asked.

"She's still on some of the drugs, but she definitely

looks stronger and happier. No more fever. I'm thinking if the tube feeds help her put on weight faster, she'll have more energy, she can start weaning off the ventilator. She should start to make more rapid progress."

"They send them home earlier now than they used to, don't they?" Kate said. A frown marred her still lovely face for a moment, and the corners of her wide mouth dropped. "I have a friend whose grandson came early and they discharged him when he only weighed around three pounds. He was on oxygen and tube feeds, and his parents had to manage all that at home. I can't imagine it. In their position, I think I'd rather trust the hospital to handle everything, even if it meant my baby staying in longer."

Across the table, Lucas's and Reba's eyes met, instantly communicating the same instinctive reaction.

No.

They wanted Maggie out of the NICU as soon as her staff thought that she and they were ready, and not one day later.

Reba felt a wave of warm reassurance at knowing the two of them shared the same feeling on this.

But then her father asked, "Is there a clock ticking on your return to New York, Lucas?"

"I'm working on it," he answered, his mouth flat and his jaw square.

And an answer like this could be interpreted in more than one way.

Was he in as much of a hurry to get back to his normal life as they both were to have Maggie discharged?

As per their timetable, he returned to the hospital after the meal, to sit with Maggie overnight. The next morning, Reba drove her parents to the airport for an emotional goodbye, then went straight to the NICU.

Lucas had obviously been impatient to see her. With the

drive out to the airport, she was a couple of hours later than usual for their private shift change. His head turned as soon as he heard her approach, and instead of staying by Maggie's isolette, he stood and came quickly toward her.

"I'm glad you're here. I kept thinking, what if the flight gets delayed? Guess what?" he said. He put his arms around her and swung her off her feet.

"Something good, I can tell."

"They're going to let us hold her this morning. Can you believe it? At last!"

"Oh, Lucas!" She dropped her forehead to his shoulder, so many emotions churning inside that they made her whole body vibrate.

"Her infection has gone, all her stats are great. She's really turned a corner, and she's almost a month old."

"Where's your mom? Will she be able to watch?"

"She phoned from her room to say she had some shopping she needed to do. I'm not going to wait any longer. Angela says now is a good time, because Maggie is awake and alert and not fussy. Let's not miss our chance."

"Our first chance," Reba corrected.

"Our first chance," he agreed, then his expression changed. "Yours. Angela says we'll have to take turns, and I've already told her it's going to be you, today. Her mom."

"Lucas…"

"Don't argue, okay? You carried her inside you all that time. You're the one whose heartbeat she wants to hear."

Reba could only nod. It made sense. Still, it was generous. He must want this milestone and this reward as much as she did. She put a hand on his arm and managed a husky, "Thanks."

They were standing very close. She brushed his cheek with her fingers, looked into his tired eyes then dropped her gaze. His mouth looked so beautiful and so familiar that she couldn't drag her eyes away and they almost kissed.

Almost.

Not quite.

Some unnamed caution held both of them back, the way the presence of their parents had held them back over the past week or more.

Angela was grinning broadly at them when they arrived back at Maggie's isolette. "Just a little bit happy about this?" she said.

"Just a little bit," Reba agreed.

"And you have a front-buttoned top on this morning, which is perfect, so let's get this show on the road before Maggie starts telling us she's too tired."

A month ago, neither Reba nor Lucas would have understood what a delicate, complex procedure it could be, just to hold their own baby. Now, because they hadn't been allowed to do it before, it seemed momentous and almost frightening. There was so much equipment to deal with, and Maggie was still so small.

Reba sat in a low chair, its stiff arms padded with pillows, while Angela detached the end of Maggie's feed tube, temporarily removed a sensor line and carefully positioned her IV and breathing equipment.

"Okay, now we want her skin-to-skin on your chest, Reba, so we need that top unfastened."

She nodded. "Uh-huh." Then she caught a wicked glint in Lucas's eye which she couldn't help reflecting right back at him.

Okay, so Maggie's not the only one who wants to get skin-to-skin with my chest…

A few minutes later, they'd both forgotten the moment of awareness, because holding Maggie was just too precious and wonderful to leave room for thoughts about anything else.

She was so warm and delicate and precious. And she was a baby. Their baby. And holding was what you did with babies. Babies and mothers were so totally meant for this. It had been so wrong and hard, not to be able to do it for so long.

Maggie's lips made little sucking sounds, and her breath smelled like honey and cream cheese. So did her hair, finer than silk, and her skin, sweeter than rose petals. She was softer than a kitten, warmer than new bread, more precious than the keys to a magic kingdom, so tiny and fragile and unique.

Lucas couldn't keep his distance, and Reba didn't want him to. He couldn't hold Maggie in his arms himself—his turn would have to wait until tomorrow—but still he could share in this. Angela found another chair for him, and positioned it hard against Reba's.

"You can put your arms around her, Lucas," she said. "Around Reba. Help her to support Maggie's little bottom. Stay that way as long as you want."

He did, and the heavy warmth of his arm and shoulder against her felt so good. Together, they "kangarooed" Maggie for nearly an hour while she slept in Reba's arms. Her heartbeat stayed strong and her oxygen sats hovered in the high nineties, but Reba didn't need the monitors to tell her that Maggie loved this, and that it would help her to thrive and grow.

It did tire her out eventually, however. She began to twitch and grimace, and her heartbeat slowed.

"We'll put her back, now," Angela whispered. "She can dream about the way you smell, Reba, and we can do it again tomorrow."

Lucas's mother appeared in the unit while they were still transferring the baby back to her isolette, and her eyes filled with tears when she hugged Reba a few minutes later.

"How wonderful," she said. "Oh, I'm so happy for you! You deserve this so much, both of you! Go and celebrate together, and let me sit with her for a while."

She almost pushed them out of the NICU, and told them not to come back for at least two hours.

"Two hours," Lucas echoed to Reba, in the elevator. "Any ideas about celebrating?"

Their eyes met, and he was already grinning. There was something giddy and dizzying and almost painfully joyful in the atmosphere between them, after the wonderful hour they'd just spent with their baby.

"A few," she admitted. "All of them back at the hotel."

"Convenient! My number one idea involves going back to the hotel." He laced his fingers behind her back and swung her around, and he was still holding her when the elevator hit ground level and opened its doors. "Feels like we're on a new track now, that she's out of the woods."

As they walked across the lobby, he began to list all of the problems Maggie had avoided, the statistics that were in her favor, now, the benefits of her new nutritional schedule, the advances in preemie care over the past few years that had helped her so much, and Reba didn't want to voice the fears she still had, or even think that maybe he was feeling *too good,* because, oh, it felt so great to be feeling good about Maggie!

How could she wish it away in either of them, how could she hold herself back, let alone Lucas?

She couldn't.

So she pulled him into a quiet little corner near the florist's store, reached up and stroked his jaw and began to kiss him instead, with the deliberate aim of distracting them both with the desire that burned inside them. It worked. The familiar heat and hardness of his body surrounded her and filled her senses, and they were so hungry for each other that the ten minute drive to the hotel seemed like fifty miles.

They kissed in the elevator, kissed along the corridor, clung to each other and kissed some more, the moment Lucas had fumbled with the key card and gotten the door of their room open. They didn't even make it to the bed.

With clothes discarded all around them on the floor, they wrapped themselves around each other as tightly as if some unseen force was trying to drag them apart, and they both felt as urgent and impatient as they would have if they'd known the world was about to end.

This was going to happen here and now.

"Let me lift you against me," Lucas said.

"Oh… Yes!"

His hands cupped her bottom, his forearms curving around her thighs, and she clung to his shoulders, bracing her back against the wall. He pushed deeply into her at once, and she was more than ready for him, crying out at the thrusting pressure, aching with the slick friction, and the sensation of being filled.

His body rippled as he moved, and his mouth swooped in to kiss her neck. She arched her back and gave him her breasts, knowing that their fullness against his hard chest would torment him and make him groan. His hips rocked back and forth harder and faster, then she felt him shudder as he attempted to hold himself back, waiting for her.

"No," she told him raggedly. "Don't stop. Don't slow."

"No, because I can't," he admitted, and thrust hard into

her again. She gasped, gripped his shoulders and flung her head to the side, fast catching up to him.

He lifted her breasts in his hands and buried his face between them, then licked her peaked nipples and covered them with his hot mouth. Bracing one hand above her head against the wall, he reached the fingers of the other between the two of them and stroked her, and her universe pulsed and quivered and went blissfully dark.

He cried out, every muscle tight and shuddering, and they held each other tightly again, too shaken to speak, too overwhelmed to move.

So fast, so elemental, so important.

Reba didn't want to let him go or open her eyes or ever come back to earth. She had tears on her cheeks. Her whole body was flooded with a precious, perfect sense of completion and rightness that she didn't have words to describe. She wanted to pin all of it down somehow, hold it against her heart, preserve it forever, but she didn't know how.

Chapter Thirteen

"**Y**ou're sorry but *what?*" Lucas said to the ground staff at the airline counter. "Delayed for almost two hours and now *what?*"

"I'm afraid, yes, the flight has been cancelled," the woman at the counter confirmed.

"And it would have to be the last flight of the day, at this hour, right?"

"Unfortunately, yes."

In an upbeat, conciliatory tone, the woman outlined Lucas's mother's choices regarding compensation for the inconvenience, and her flight options for the following day, while Lucas reminded himself that despite the better days he and Reba and Maggie had been having for the past week or more, he was still chronically tired and chronically stressed, that an airline's obsessive concern for mechanical safety checks was a good thing, and that it really wouldn't help to yell.

At his elbow, while her flight was being rescheduled by the click of computer keys, Mom kept apologizing. "I should have thought not to choose the last flight of the day, Lucas. I'll take a cab out here tomorrow."

"No need, because I'm meeting Dad off his flight at ten," Lucas said.

"Ah. We'll overlap."

"Can you handle that?"

"I'm not going to throw a tantrum over it. He might. In his own unique way." She sighed. "This is probably for the best. We shouldn't try to avoid each other. Not when we're grandparents to the same child."

"You're parents to the same child, too," he pointed out mildly.

"Hmm. True. We did the best we could at the time, Lucas. I'm sorry. I know it wasn't always enough."

"One thing I've meant to ask, actually. Did you have anything to do with this visit of his? He'd told me he wasn't coming until Maggie was…" He hesitated over the right word. *Presentable?* No, better to stay as neutral as possible. "Healthy and growing and out of danger. But then she got the infection. Was that what changed his mind? Or was it something you said?"

"The infection changed *my* mind. So I called and yelled at him. I told him for once in his life he had to commit to something even when it wasn't providing an appropriate return on his investment—"

"You mean even when it hurt?"

"Exactly. And I told him that he'd already done you enough damage with his serial bail outs."

"Damage?" Lucas echoed, a little surprised. Shocked, even. "To me?"

"Yes, to you."

The desk attendant finished at her computer and told them, "All fixed up for tomorrow at one forty-five."

They thanked her, and before they walked away Lucas's mother cupped his cheek in the kind of caress he hadn't let her give him in years. She looked into his eyes.

"Don't you think?" she said gently. "Oh, I know he's always been so scrupulous in some areas. Never began a new affair until he'd already walked out of the marriage. Always made it clear from the beginning if he was promising a quick fling with the right gifts attached, or the more dubious gift of a wedding band. Generous with alimony and property settlements."

"He always told me that was the correct and decent way to handle it."

"Yes, but that still didn't make all those rapid-fire marriages and divorces and serial short-term flings *right.* Not really. And as a result he's somehow left you with the idea that life—and relationships—and feelings—are all much more *boxable* than they really are."

"Boxable? Now you're making up words."

"Are you telling me you don't know what I mean?"

"No, I guess I'm not," he answered slowly. "I guess I do know. But if I have been damaged by all that, Maggie's undoing the damage pretty fast."

"She is? Tiny Maggie?"

"Maggie and Reba," he corrected reluctantly. "Nothing in my life is *boxable* now. It's scary. It's horrible. And yet it's weird. There's a weird way in which I'm going to be… not thankful for this, but—"

"You're going to look back and understand and value exactly what you've learned."

"I think so. I hope so. But let's not...uh...count the return on the investment just yet."

They drove back to the hotel and checked Mom into a new room for one more night, then Lucas went to keep his usual nightlong vigil at the hospital, not as concerned about his parents coming face to face with each other tomorrow as he would once have been.

Mom was probably right. It would probably be a good thing. And with Maggie hovering like an unspoken blessing in the background, they'd handle it in the right way.

Meanwhile, his tiny daughter almost looked as if she was smiling in her sleep.

Lucas's father arrived as scheduled the next morning, and he and Lucas's mother and Lucas himself spent an hour and a half having coffee together in the airport bar. It wasn't exactly a joyful family reunion, but it was civilized and surprisingly pleasant all the same.

They talked about Maggie until Lucas's father said, "Can we wait until I've seen her? None of this will make real sense until I do."

Then he asked Mom about her clothing boutique and they talked business. Dad even had a couple of constructive suggestions to make regarding its expansion. Finally, Mom said firmly that she'd be fine on her own from now until her flight, and the two of them should get to the hotel for Dad to check in and to the hospital to see Maggie.

Dad's face tightened at this point, as if the business talk had allowed him to forget the reason for his visit, but when it came to the crunch he was actually okay about it— helped, no doubt, by the fact that Maggie seemed so much stronger now. He looked at her and touched her and smiled. He sat beside her for an hour at a stretch, twice in two days. He was courteous to the nurses, and didn't say the wrong thing to Reba.

He studied Reba a little as if she was a horse whose bloodlines he had to check out, but apparently they were bloodlines he approved of, on closer analysis.

"You did well," he told Lucas on the final morning of his visit, as they had breakfast together at the hotel. Reba had already gone to the hospital.

"Yeah?" Lucas answered. "In what area?"

"Well, if you're going to have a baby with a woman you've got no intention of marrying, you could have done a lot worse. This one is bright and strong and loving. Maggie will have some good qualities in her make up."

Yep, it was about bloodlines.

"She's not a thoroughbred racer, Dad, and neither is Reba."

"Well, she should be, in your eyes. A man with your background and your prospects should look at potential mothers for his children with an eye to the right attributes, just like a stud breeder does."

"I'll take that on board, Dad…"

"Do!"

A few weeks later, Maggie celebrated her two month birthday by nudging her weight up over 1,300 grams.

Her parents thought she was absolutely, fantastically, wonderfully huge, and brilliantly clever for digesting all that lovely breast milk coming through her naso-gastric tube without any of the gut problems her doctor had warned them about. Another sixty grams, and she would weigh three pounds, according to the weird, unfamiliar baby measurement system that the parents of nonpreemies unaccountably preferred to use when discussing their gargantuan offspring.

She was getting longer, and less scrunched up, her skin was not so translucent and red, and her black preemie hair was falling out to make way for her real hair to show its color later on. Would she be a brunette, a redhead or a blonde? With all three groups represented somewhere on both sides of the family, it was anyone's guess.

She'd been taken off the ventilator, and that was a huge step, but she still needed supplemental oxygen through a tube in her nose. Soon, she would start to wean from that and onto room air.

Somewhat to her own astonishment, Reba had become a poster girl for the success of the pump, and she'd almost forgotten that there was any other way to do it—until Angela told her one morning, when Maggie hit 1,320 grams, "We're going to see if she's strong enough to nipple some of her feeds, now."

"Nipple them?"

"Yep. Direct from Mom."

Oh. Right.

Yikes.

She didn't know whether to wish that Lucas was here, or to feel thoroughly relieved that he wasn't. They'd been keeping strictly to their timetable since his father's departure. Reba did days. Lucas did nights. Around twelve hours each.

The only thing that changed was that as Maggie grew and got healthier, their nursing shift-change equivalents in their hotel suite had tended to get longer. And steamier. And more relaxing and—and—*funnier,* actually, because they'd remembered how to laugh, just lately, and it felt so nice.

They went out, sometimes, too. Little snatches of another life. Ice-cream, or shopping. Greenery and fresh air. More laughter.

Lucas probably would have laughed at Reba's first direct nipple-to-mouth breastfeeding attempt, if he'd been here to see it. She and Maggie were both in tears by the time they threw in the towel.

And towels literally were involved—and were thrown—because it got messy, and wet, and—

No. Don't obsess about it.

"You did real well, honey," Angela told her. "And so did Maggie."

Reba gave a helpless laugh. "Oh, yeah, I bet you say that to all the girls."

"No, I'm serious. It was your first time, both of you, and her mouth is still so little, and she's never felt it all full of milk, so she panicked a bit and couldn't work out how to suck and swallow in sequence. It's really hard when she's never done it before. We'll get our lactation consultant in, next time. Want to keep holding her for a while?"

"Can I?"

"She loves it, now. It'll calm her and relax her again. She's a bit tense."

"So's her mom!"

"Want to change her diaper and give her a little wash, later on?"

"Now there, I'm a seasoned performer!"

It was really pretty amazing how quickly the day went by. In the afternoon, after Maggie had had a good, peaceful sleep and woken up to look alert and happy, they tried the nipple-to-mouth thing again with the lactation consultant in attendance, and made a little progress. For about a minute, Maggie looked as if she was getting the idea and liked it, but then she choked and got upset, and by the time

Reba could soothe her again she'd gotten tired and gone back to sleep.

"But Angela and Helen both tell me I'm doing well, and I guess they wouldn't say it if it wasn't true," she reported to Lucas back at the hotel that evening.

They celebrated the milestone with a three-course room service feast, including champagne, and got a little giddy. Lucas opened the window to let in the spring air, then put on the radio and found some 1930s big band swing music, and they pretended that they knew how to dance to it, swirling each other around, ending up just clinging to each other, whirling, dizzy and laughing.

Dangerous.

Even while it was happening, Reba somehow knew it was dangerous.

They were both too wired, too wound up, too intense. Because let's face it, they were still sleeping badly, their nerves were still stretched thin, thin, thin. It almost seemed normal, now, to be running on empty like this.

And a baby had died in the NICU today. Reba hadn't told Lucas, but he'd find out soon enough. The little boy had had severe birth defects and everyone had known it was just a matter of time. In fact it was almost a relief. Still, it broke your heart. And it scared you.

Thinking about it again, Reba pulled Lucas to a halt in the middle of whirling each other across the floor, looked into his face and said, "I'm superstitious. Let's not dance. Not yet."

She reached over to the remote control on the table and switched the radio off with a click.

He sobered up at once. She loved the shape of his mouth when it was steady like this, even though she'd loved his glowing grin, too. "The roller coaster?" he said.

"The roller coaster. I'm at the top of the ride and my heart is pounding, wondering where the track goes next."

"She's doing great though, isn't she?"

He touched her face, brushing the hair back from her forehead, soothing the frown lines, tracing her lips. Coming through the open window from the hotel conference center ballroom at ground level below, they could still hear music in the clear spring air, and Reba recognized the haunting, slow-dance beat of "Unchained Melody."

"Is it really so wrong to celebrate?" Lucas went on. "To let ourselves go, just for a bit?" His body still swayed to the lazy, three-beat rhythm they could hear. "You're the emotional one, Reba. Shouldn't you applaud me for loosening my reins, for not acting so rational, for once? You should be telling me you're surprised I even know how to dance."

"Neither of us knows how to dance. Neither of us is—" She stopped and shook her head, not really sure what she wanted to say, or why she felt like this. She *was* the emotional one. Why did she suddenly want to rein it in?

Maybe because feeding Maggie today hadn't exactly been a success, despite the nurses' encouragement. Maybe because she'd felt relaxed enough to take more notice of what was going on elsewhere in the unit, and had remembered babies who'd crashed at various times over the past few months.

Most of those babies had climbed back up to greater health and strength, but some of them hadn't. And when the nurses talked about those babies, they most often talked about feelings in their gut, not figures on a chart.

What was her gut saying to her about Maggie?

"Hey," Lucas said, still holding her, swinging her slowly back and forth in his arms, not quite dancing, but almost.

He felt so strong and upright and just *right* against her body. Familiar. Complex, but she was starting to understand his complexities, now. "I'm not going to let you get some irrational fear thing going here, and ruin our evening."

"Talk me out of it, then, Lucas. Please?"

"There's no reason to get superstitious. We love her, and she knows it, and if I never would have believed a couple of months ago that our love has the power to help her, I believe it now. So let's dance."

"No..." But her body kept moving in time to his, even while she made the half-hearted protest.

"Then let's make love," he whispered. "It's almost the same thing..."

He held her as if ready for a waltz, dipped her in his arms until she was off-balance, swooped her up close again. He ran his hands down her back and kissed her neck, heating her skin with warm breath, still moving and swaying. "Let me make you forget everything, because you're seeing stars."

"Yes..."

The words sung by the live band drifted up to them and rang so true that the music seemed to be playing just for them.

Yes.

She hungered for his touch.

She needed his love.

He slid his hands down her body, pausing at her hips to pull her closer against him, rocking to the slow beat. His mouth travelled lower, touching, claiming, reminding her of their power over each other and their need for each other with every imprint on her skin. Slowly, erotically, like a private tandem strip routine, he shed her clothing and his until they were both naked, every pore and every nerve-ending sensitized, every touch unraveling them a little further.

"So are we dancing, or making love?" he whispered. "Tell me, Reba."

"Both," she whispered back. "I've lost track. You said it—is there really a difference?"

"No. Not with you. All the boundaries disappear when I'm with you."

Through the window, the song changed, and changed again, but the rhythm and the emotion stayed the same— slow and heartfelt and sensual. He touched her intimately while they danced, kissed her breasts and knelt to wrap her swaying hips with his arms before moving his mouth lower. She gasped and the strength melted from her legs. They both fell to the floor, locked together, throbbing with need.

When he thrust into her, with her body arched high on top of his and her legs straddling his hard male bulk, she was so ready that she cried out at once, over and over, and her pleasure made his own urgency surge in response, bringing them both to a climax within a few short minutes. When they came back to earth and held each other, breathing together, Reba felt shaken to the core and deeply aware of how vulnerable she was, in so many ways.

So many ways.

Maggie's temperature spiked upward four days later.

"Where's Lucas? Is he here?" Reba said, not caring how urgent she sounded.

"No, he's not, honey," Angela answered, frowning, against the usual background of morning NICU noise and activity. Sinks ran with water. Monitor alarms went off. Ventilators pulled and pushed whooshes of air. "He left around the same time as usual. Eight o'clock, an hour after I came on. He didn't come back to the hotel to have breakfast with you?"

The nurses were thoroughly on top of Reba's and Lucas's private routine, by this time. Angela looked at her watch and frowned again. It was ten-thirty, now—a good hour later than Reba usually came in.

Lucas hadn't showed up at their suite after his nightly vigil. Reba had waited, starting to sweat as the clock ticked over toward eight-thirty. He'd usually arrived by this time. She had phoned the unit and spoken to one of the doctor's, who'd told her that Maggie's condition hadn't changed during the night.

She wasn't getting worse, after thirty-six hours under this latest threat to her health, but she wasn't getting better, either.

Another major infection had taken hold, Dr. Charleson had concluded. They'd taken blood and urine samples for testing. They'd begun to zap her with antibiotics. They'd put her back onto levels of treatment that Reba and Lucas had   stupidly—dangerously—unforgivably—assumed were done and gone.

Those treatments were for other babies, now, not theirs. They were for other parents to suffer over. Reba and Lucas and Maggie had been through it already. They'd been through so much. More than enough. Hadn't they had their full share?

So where was he?

If he wasn't at the hotel, why wasn't he here?

"How is she?" Reba asked, turning to bend close to Maggie.

She couldn't really see her. Her eyes were too blurred with panicky tears. Five and a half days ago, she and Lucas had celebrated Maggie's first real feed with that crazy dancing in each other's arms, and lovemaking that had swept her to the heights, cradled her in bliss and floated her back to earth. Now they were plunged into fear and torment again.

If Reba herself had managed to grab a couple of hours of fractured sleep over the past two nights during the quiet of the early hours, she didn't think Lucas had even tried during his daytime breaks. On top of everything else, he must be on the point of collapse.

"She's about the same," Angela reported reluctantly. "I couldn't say she's turned a corner, yet."

"But she's not getting worse?"

"She goes up and down. The medication isn't bringing her temperature down quite as far as we want." She took a careful breath. "Dr. Charleson is considering a lumbar puncture."

And Reba had been around the NICU for over two months now. She knew this was bad, and she knew why. "Meningitis?" She'd seen another family going through it—two anguished parents and their very ill baby—and they'd gotten a positive result on the test. That little girl was still struggling for life.

Her throat squeezed tight shut. "Does Lucas know about this?"

"Yes, Dr. Charleson discussed it with him first thing this morning."

"Wh-when will Dr. Charleson make the decision? When will he do it?"

"He's going to give her another few hours to start responding to the medication."

"Why doesn't he do it now? What if he leaves it too late?"

Angela's reply was so unlike her normal clear responses that Reba couldn't even make sense of it at first, then she understood.

"You mean, even if it is meningitis, you're already doing pretty much all you can?"

Again, Angela's answer was just a meaningless jumble

of sounds, with a couple of words standing out. Something about "heroic measures," but Reba knew that Maggie was the only heroic one here right now.

She endured an agonizing two hours, watching her feverish, struggling baby—wasn't she looking just a little bit better, by the end of it?—but Lucas still didn't show. Finally she managed to tear herself away. Calling their hotel suite, she got the ringing tone then the hotel's message service inviting her to speak after the tone. The front desk told her, a minute later, that he hadn't left a written message.

Did she know how to dial in to her suite's voice mail to retrieve any messages there?

No, she didn't.

Laboriously, she noted the desk clerk's instructions and managed to press the right buttons to check, but there was nothing.

How could this be happening?

In desperation, she checked the cafeteria, the parents' room and even hammered on a couple of hospital men's room doors, but he wasn't anywhere. She would have called his mother in Beverly Hills, only she didn't want to scare Kate any more than the news of Maggie's fresh infection had already scared her yesterday.

She did call the ranch, but the hands were all hard at work and no one picked up.

Crazy to call, anyhow. Why on earth would Lucas be there?

Back at Maggie's isolette, Phil Charleson studied the baby and her chart, then looked up when he saw her coming. His eyes seemed clouded with thought. Or fatigue. His wife was right. He never seemed to go home.

"Have you—" Her voice dried up completely and she had to clear her throat and gulp the water Angela handed her before she could speak again. "Have you decided on the lumbar puncture yet, Dr. Charleson?"

"Not going to do it," he said decisively. Then he smiled. "She's turned the corner on this, just over the past couple of hours. Her symptoms didn't fit with meningitis from the beginning, but then she was slow to respond to treatment and there was a point where I had some doubts. Occasionally meningitis presents in an atypical way. Not this time, I'm happy to say."

Reba's relief washed over her so strongly that she had to sit down or she would have simply collapsed. "That's— Oh, I'm so—" No one needed her to complete a coherent sentence at this point, so she gave up and concentrated on simply remembering to breathe.

But Lucas still wasn't here.

And Maggie was still sick.

"We're not going to let her drop the ball, Reba," Angela said. "We're going to support her all the way. She should beat this with antibiotics. She's stronger than she was, even a couple of weeks ago."

Lucas didn't have the same confidence; was that why he wasn't here?

"I'm going to go back to the hotel," Reba said.

She'd had to take a cab to the hospital this morning, because Lucas had the SUV. Somewhere, he had it. Where?

Now she took another cab back again, but their suite was still empty and silent. The light on the telephone blinked, however, and when she played the message, she heard his voice, distorted with emotion and almost drowned by background noise.

She could only make out one part of what he said.

"I need some space."

That was it.

Space.

How much? Where had he gone to find it? And did he ever plan on coming back?

She left a written message for him on the desk, and an angry verbal one on their voice mail, in case he called in to check.

"Don't do this. I couldn't hear all of your message. I don't know where you are. I don't know anything. Maggie is still sick. They're not doing a lumbar puncture. It's not meningitis. But she's still sick and—" And I just don't want to go through this alone. She couldn't say it, because she *was* alone, and she might have to get used to it. "No, never mind," she finished.

On her way out, the attendant at the concierge desk spotted her and called her over. He had the keys to the SUV in his hands. "Someone just delivered these for you, Miss Grant. I was about to leave a message on your voice mail."

"Delivered the keys?"

"And the car. Mr. Halliday wanted it driven back here from the airport."

"From the airport," Reba echoed. "Do you—do you have any further information than that?"

"I'm sorry, I don't. Is there a problem?"

A problem? Just one?

How much time do you have to listen, and where shall I start?

Hiding her turmoil, she answered, "No, it's fine. Thanks." She took the keys, put them in her purse, and digested the meager amount of new information. He'd gone to the airport. That could only mean he'd left Denver.

When she got back to the hospital, Carla was there.

"You pick the best days!" she told her friend shakily,

then seeing Carla's alarmed expression, she added at once, "No, I'm not going to yell at you. I need you too much."

"Where's Lucas?"

She sketched out what she knew, and Carla didn't know what to say. "He wouldn't just—"

"Go back to New York? He might. He probably has. Why not? We're both cracking up, Carla. This latest thing with Maggie, just when we thought she was—" hard to even say the word without mocking their foolish innocence "—safe. I don't know what he'd do, any more. I don't know what he feels, if he could disappear like this."

"Feels about you?"

"Feels about anything."

"And how do you feel?"

"Don't ask me that now."

Because I love him.

With all the differences between us, all the ways we've misunderstood each other, and even though he isn't here, I love him. I'm scared for him, too scared to be angry, and I'm angry anyhow, but I'm scared about what might be happening inside him, right now, and it hurts too much to put any of the whole mess into words.

"So let's go get some lunch," Carla said. "You're a mother. You have to eat. What do you want?"

"Well, some shredded cardboard might be nice."

"Yes. Good choice. Yum."

"That's all anything is going to taste like."

But in the end it wasn't so bad. She chose pasta because it was easiest to chew, and Carla caught her up on news from Biggins, including the fact that Gordie McConnell's ranch had been sold.

"Do you know who bought it?"

"Some outfit with a corporate name, apparently. The deal's not finalized yet."

"Gordie's still living there?"

"Honey, you haven't heard why it was on the market, have you?" Carla said, reaching across the table to lay a hand on hers.

"No."

"It only came out once we heard that the place had sold. He racked up huge debts trading shares on the Internet, and couldn't get out from under. It started out as legitimate trading, but it turned into a gambling problem in the end. He was throwing money into all these dubious concerns, trying to recoup his losses." She stopped and shook her head. "Bad decisions, all the way. He's on someone's spread up north, now, as foreman. Might not have happened if he'd gotten on with his life properly, instead of hanging after you."

"Oh, my fault?"

"Not your fault. His fault. For not knowing when you meant what you said."

"Maybe that isn't his fault." Reba shook her head helplessly. "Maybe it's mine."

"Hey…"

"I always mean what I say. I say what's in my heart. But sometimes it changes. Am I inconsistent, or something? You know, blowing hot and cold. Maybe Gordie had every right to think I'd come round, because when I said no, it was just another mood."

"No, Reba. That's not what you're like. You're pretty passionate, sometimes, but—"

"Lucas and I talk about the roller coaster. With Maggie. The heart-in-your-mouth ups and downs that are pulling us to pieces. Did I do that to Gordie?"

"*No,* Reba! This is his problem, not yours."

"Do I do it to Lucas? Have I done it to him? Is that why—?"

"No. That's not why he's disappeared. I can't believe that, and you mustn't, either. You have enough you're taking on without taking on that responsibility as well. Think about what counts. What counts for you right now, Reba?"

"Maggie and Lucas. That's all, Carla. Really that's all, right now. Maggie and Lucas."

"You don't think he's just walked out of your life, do you, and that he's not coming back? Would he do that? Think. Think about the people who really count—and you're right, that's Maggie and Lucas, it's not Gordie. Maggie and Lucas, Reba. You know him pretty well now. Maybe you can work it out."

"Maggie…" Reba put her fork down in her empty plate. "I'm going back to sit with her, again."

"I'm going to make sure you get there in one piece."

"I still have legs, Carla, and I know the way, by this time."

"Legs look a little shaky today, hon."

"Today? They've been shaky for two months!"

"And I'll stay overnight here if you want. I can call Chris."

Reba hugged her. "That's so good of you. I'm not going to let you do it. But just the fact that you offered… You have your little guys, Carla. Go home and hug them for me, and love them, and be so happy that they're strong."

"You're strong, too," Carla answered. "You can get through this."

Chapter Fourteen

In his first-class airplane seat on the flight to Hawaii, Lucas stretched, lay back and appreciated the comfort of the leather upholstery and the taste of the fine wine. A flight attendant offered a selection of gourmet European cheeses and when he nodded and smiled, she set the plate on a starched linen napkin on the wide tray in front of him. A pretty little arrangement of dewy purple grapes and lush red strawberries complemented the paler tones of the cheese.

Yes, this felt good.

It did.

This was his real life again, at last. Luxury and deference. Success and control. His laptop in its customized case, ready for when he wanted to work. Personal screen and headset, and a program of movies and TV shows, music and video games, so he could shut out the world and tune in to whatever electronic escape he chose.

He'd left a voice mail message for Reba from the airport, he'd arranged for the SUV to be delivered to the hotel, where she had everything else she needed on tap, and the way he felt right now, the message and the vehicle acquitted him of any further obligation and responsibility.

Because what good did it do, to be with the people you cared about? To take responsibility for them? What the hell good did it do? What good did it do to care about them in the first place? At all? What garbage had he told Reba, less than a week ago, about their love for their baby and its power to help her?

He'd spent more than two months with Maggie. Two long months of slow, slow torture. Thinking about her every minute, staying just a few feet from her for hours and hours of every day, watching every breath, every movement, every figure on her monitors and in her charts.

He'd loved her so much, poured *so much* love into her that he'd astonished himself at the capacity he had for it. To love a baby that much. To love a creature who hadn't even existed eight months ago *that much*. To love someone who couldn't even smile.

And what the hell good had it done? For Maggie, or for Reba or for Lucas himself?

And if it didn't do any good, if all that painful, hardworking, totally committed, faithful, optimistic, exhausting love had had zero power to help her when it came to the crunch, if the only things that had helped her—and then had cruelly let her down—were simply modern medicine and blind luck, then why the hell put himself through it any more? Why the hell put Maggie through it? Maybe she'd hated having him sitting there, hour after hour, bombarding her with all that stressed out, useless love.

So why not go to Hawaii?

Yeah.

He'd never been, and he'd heard it was a pretty nice place. Beaches. Jungles. Volcanoes. Beautiful women wearing hula skirts on their hips and strings of flowers round their necks. Big, punch-packing candy-flavored drinks in hollowed out pineapples with colorful bendy straws and paper umbrellas sticking out the top.

Yeah.

Some of that, thanks.

Enough with love.

I'm going to enjoy my fine selection of European cheeses and watch the movie of my choice.

Yeah.

And I don't know when I'm coming back.

Angela stood back a little, once she'd gotten Maggie safely positioned in Reba's arms. Lactation consultant Sarah Emery would be helping mother and baby learn to breastfeed successfully, today, following the hiatus during Maggie's latest illness, and Angela knew that Sarah was very good at what she did.

"She should be here in a couple of minutes," she told Reba. "She got delayed on the phone."

Maggie's infection had cleared up beautifully, over the past couple of days. Looking at her, you wouldn't have known she'd been such a sick baby girl just four days earlier. Another day or two, and Dr. Charleson would probably downgrade her from one-to-one nursing status and move her to another section of the unit. Another week or two, and they'd start to talk about her discharge.

In fact, the setback had taken its toll on Reba and Lucas far more than on their daughter.

Lucas had apparently disappeared off the face of the

earth, and Reba seemed painfully split between anger and concern. The inevitable exhaustion, too. With Lucas absent, she only ever left the hospital to snatch a few hours sleep overnight. Angela planned to order her back to the hotel for a decent lunch and a nap, once this feeding session was over.

Reba was clearly thinking about Lucas right now, her face dropped into a narrow-eyed, tight-mouthed shape that tore at Angela's heart. She could have yelled at Lucas…if she hadn't understood that he was probably already doing himself quite a lot more damage than mere yelling from a nurse would inflict.

As if Reba could read minds, she looked up from the little bundle that was Maggie, and said to Angela in a shaky voice, "I mean, does this happen? Do preemie dads do this? Is it a—a syndrome, or something? I want it to be. I'm just like Lucas! I want to look it up on the Internet and print out pages of relevant data. Vanishingpreemiedads.net or something. All the statistics. The relationship survival rate. The percentage of dads who show up after three days. The percentage who never come back at all. Or is he the only one who's ever done it?"

One of those questions no nursing degree could ever qualify you to answer. As usual, because you just had to, Angela tried to answer it anyhow.

"We do get parents who disappear, sometimes," she said carefully. The ones who were young, scared and alone. The ones with problems. The ones with addictions. "Moms and dads. But not fathers like Lucas. He was so involved with Maggie, Reba, I can't see him turning into a long-term deadbeat dad, just like that. He'll be back. Question is when."

"Question is, am I angry!"

"Well, sure you're angry."

Reba let out a breathy sound. "Oh. Angela. Thanks for saying it!" She blinked back tears. "Thanks so much for just coming right out and saying it! Yes. I'm angry. I'm *angry*," she repeated, as if the license to speak the words out loud was the best freedom she'd been given in days.

It probably was.

The NICU could feel like a prison, sometimes.

A parent's emotions could feel like one, too.

And Lucas was a prison escapee.

"Do you think that's permanent, honey?" Angela asked. "Will you forgive him, when he shows up? How strong is your love?"

"I'm so sorry," Sarah Emery said, arriving at that moment. "I couldn't cut short that call. Is she still awake? Oh, sweetheart, yes, you're looking wonderfully alert and ready for this, aren't you, little girl? Let's get started."

Over Sarah's head, as she bent toward Maggie, Angela saw Reba scrape her teeth across her bottom lip, then turn down her mouth and give a tight little shrug that seemed to say, "How strong is my love? I wish I knew."

They looked like a painting of the Madonna and Child, Lucas thought, as soon as he saw Reba and Maggie.

Beautiful.

Perfect.

It had taken him a full minute to find them, because Maggie's isolette had been moved. When he'd first looked over to the familiar corner, on entering the unit, and had seen a different baby there—a very sick baby—with a different nurse in attendance, he'd experienced instant darkness across his vision and had almost blacked out.

But then the nurse had looked up, taken in the way he was gripping the nearest chair-back with desperate fingers and told him, "You're Maggie's Dad, right? She's on the far side of the unit, now. She doesn't need this level of care anymore."

"Because she's—" His husky voice had dried up completely.

"Doing so well."

And she was. He could see it from here. They were both doing so well. Reba had the baby's mouth at her breast and was smiling down at her. Maggie had her eyes closed, but her little cheeks were moving rhythmically as she sucked, and if that wasn't bliss on her face, then the word had no meaning in any dictionary.

Reba hadn't seen him yet, even though he'd moved closer. She was too absorbed. She had her finger resting lightly against Maggie's cheek and she was smiling, so happy.

Complete.

The two of them looked so complete together, and Lucas's heart twisted and climbed into the back of his throat. Painful. Uncomfortable. Nauseating.

What had he done?

He'd gone away, abandoned them.

Five whole days.

Five days of tramping Hawaiian beaches, brooding into black cups of coffee at outdoor tropical cafes. He'd even climbed a volcano.

Because why not climb a volcano, when love had no power?

Except he'd discovered that it did. He still…almost… didn't want it to, but it just did.

Love might not do Maggie or Reba or himself any good, but it burned inside him night and day anyhow, and it wouldn't go away, and against all logic and good sense it was important—vitally, agonizingly important—and in the end he'd checked out of his private eco-cabin at the most luxurious resort on Oahu and taken the first flight he could get, back to Denver, to the two people he loved most in the world.

One of them might not have survived his absence.

The other might never forgive it.

But here he was.

He cleared his throat.

"Hi, Reba, hi, Maggie," he said.

Reba's face drained of both color and expression, and she didn't speak. They looked at each other, frozen, and he knew that all he could do was try to tell her the truth—and doing that depended completely on her willingness to hear him out.

"I bailed, didn't I?" he began.

Her eyes narrowed, and she looked angry, vulnerable, searching, all at the same time. "Are you going to tell me about it?" she said, with less emotion than he'd expected.

"If you'll listen."

"I'm not going anywhere, right now, with a baby on my lap."

"She looks fabulous. Bigger. She's feeding, and she's not choking."

"We've been having lessons. We're A students, now."

His voice shrank to a whisper. "I've missed her so much. Missed you, even more."

"Funny, I don't remember the postcard in which you mentioned that."

"I tore up the postcard."

"You actually wrote one?"

"I wanted to write about a hundred. Couldn't pick up a pen or a telephone or—Reba, I cracked. I was so angry at the universe for playing such terrible tricks on my heart. All that love I poured into her, and she got sick again, and

I just filled up with stubbornness and despair. I wasn't going to love her, damn it, if that was the reward. I wasn't going to love you, because some day I'd get rewarded for that in the same terrible, painful way."

Her face stayed still and watchful. "So you left."

"I left. I went to Hawaii. Climbed a volcano."

"Lovely!"

"It wasn't. Well, it is. It's beautiful. But it was hell for me."

Reba exploded, as much as a woman could explode when she had a tiny, precious baby on her lap. "Hell for you?" she mouthed, like someone shouting on TV with the sound turned down. "Do you have the slightest idea what it's been like for me?"

"Yes. Yes, sweetheart, I do. Impossible. Agonizing. I know. The same agony of not knowing that we've both endured for more than two months, and that made me crack up in the end, that made me just refuse to do it any more."

"To do what?"

"To feel the love. I was fighting so hard. I didn't *want* to feel any of this. For five whole days I tried to force myself not to feel it, but…" He spread his hands. "I just do feel it, Reba. I love her. And I love you. So much. You remember when we were at the cabin I said you got swept up in currents of emotion and had no control over where you were washed up?"

"I remember," she admitted.

"That same current swept me up and carried me along and washed me up…just loving you, loving both of you. Loving you until my heart almost shattered with it. And I want it, now. I can't live without it. Can you forgive what I had to do, to find that out?"

Oh, could she? After an explanation like that?

Reba didn't quite know if she was laughing or crying.

So Lucas thought that she was the emotional one? He had to climb a volcano in Hawaii in order to understand his own heart, and he thought *she* was the emotional one?

"Yes, I can forgive you," she said, because she had no choice. She'd had no choice from day one, where this man was concerned! The current of her emotions had brought her to this point weeks ago. She loved him, and as he did, she had no say in the matter at all. "I forgive you, Lucas. I love you. So much. My heart is bursting."

Okay, so she was crying. She must be, because he was brushing tears from her face, and his eyes glistened and blurred and brimmed just like hers did.

"Marry me, too?" he whispered. "Make us a family— you, Maggie and me?"

"On the advice of your lawyer, the way it was before?"

"No, to save my heart, because it's bursting, too."

"Then I'd better say yes."

"Can I hear it? Can you say it?"

"Yes, Lucas. Oh, yes, I'll marry you as soon as you want!"

He bent toward her, because they both wanted to seal the moment with a kiss, but Maggie had something to say about that. She choked on her milk and started to splutter, so Reba gently eased her breast away, lifted the baby up, checked that she could breathe, and wiped her mouth.

"Better now, sweetheart?" she whispered, smiling at Maggie because she just couldn't stop smiling at Maggie, lately. "Sorry about that, little girl. But your mommy and daddy have decided to get married, which feels pretty nice, and, well— Oh!"

Maggie was smiling back.

She was.

An unmistakable, wide-mouthed, bright-eyed, milky, beautiful, heavenly smile.

"Angela?" Lucas said in a shaky voice, and the nurse came over. "Is this possible? Look, Maggie's smiling! Surely that's not possible. In gestational age, she's still not born yet."

"It's perfectly possible, and she's definitely doing it," Angela said. "Preemies see smiling faces when other babies are still in the womb. They learn from what they see, and so they start early. Was Mommy smiling at you, sweetheart? Is Mommy feeling good about something right now?"

"I was smiling at her. I am. I can't stop. I'm so happy," Reba said. "We're getting married, Angela! We're giving Maggie a family."

Angela grinned. "Oh, we've been hoping! Honey, excuse me, I'm going to go put that on Maggie's chart! I'm so thrilled for you both!"

Maggie seemed pretty happy about it, too. Absolutely beaming, with a twinkle like starlight in her eyes.

Lucas put his arm around both of them and told his daughter, "Your mommy and I are going to kiss each other now. You can keep smiling or you can stop, but you can't splutter another mouthful of milk, because I haven't kissed Mommy for nearly a week and that's way too long." He brushed Reba's lips with his and she closed her eyes, giving herself to the touch and taste she loved. "Way, way too long…" he whispered, then he deepened the kiss until time stopped.

Ten minutes later, Angela snatched a moment to make a rare phone call to Shirley and Helen at home, with the news about Maggie's parents that she knew they wouldn't want to wait to hear.

Just about two weeks after this, on a Saturday, Lucas and Reba took Maggie home. Because she wouldn't be close to a hospital, she'd been kept in the unit until fully weaned from tube feeds and oxygen, but she was getting bigger and stronger so fast, now, that the weaning had happened over a matter of days.

They were heading for Reba's little house in Biggins, but that wouldn't count as home for long. Lucas had cashed in enough of his Halliday Corporation shares to buy the McConnell ranch and take over Seven Mile from his father. He'd put both purchases in motion the time they'd gone to the cabin to take a break two months ago, intending at minimum to create a stable home base for Maggie to grow up in, where her mom would be happy.

Now, his plans for the combined ranches had changed a little. He would maintain a role in the family corporation, but his home base would be at Seven Mile, where a Swiss-style chalet and an eight thousand square foot log cabin were no longer on the construction program.

Taking Maggie home took all day.

Lucas and Reba had to check out of their hotel suite, handle the hospital discharge formalities and say goodbye to some pretty important people before driving north. Maggie needed two stops for feeding on the way. When she was hungry, she sure let her parents know it! To Reba and Lucas, the strength and volume of her cry was almost like music. Both times, after she'd fed, she slept contentedly again, strapped in her infant seat.

Even after this, there were another two stops they'd planned to make—the local county clerk's office to pick up their marriage license and change into their wedding clothes, and then the church in Biggins where they were going to be married.

Somehow, it had just seemed right that Maggie should arrive home to the ranch with her parents already man and wife, and had seemed completely unimportant, under the circumstances, for them to have a big, splashy wedding with a lot of guests in attendance.

Arriving at the church, they found a lot of guests in attendance anyhow.

"What has Carla done?" Reba murmured, as they pulled into the filled parking lot adjacent to the church.

Nervously, she took Lucas's hand and felt his answering squeeze. It sent all the usual messages to her senses, and her nervousness subsided. Beside each other and united like this, an out-of-control wedding day hardly seemed like a problem.

Confusing, maybe, but not in a bad way.

"We asked her and Chris to come and act as our witnesses," she went on, "but—"

"Seems like they've brought along a few witnesses of their own."

"A few witnesses?" She started to laugh helplessly. "It looks like the whole town!"

She saw most of the staff from the Longhorn Steakhouse, the ranch hands and their girlfriends and wives, Carla and Chris, their kids and their parents. And then she saw Maggie's nurses Shirley and Helen and Angela, dressed to the nines in outfits that definitely weren't hospital scrubs and each on the arm of their husbands.

The crowd began to disappear inside the church as Reba and Lucas unstrapped Maggie from her car seat and nestled her into a soft pink cotton baby sling that would keep her snug and protected against Reba's chest, precious girl.

There were just a few people still waiting outside as they approached, and to Reba's astonishment she recognized Kate and Farrer Halliday, standing together and smiling, and that was…yes…Mom, in her wheelchair, right beside Dad.

They'd come all this way.

Carla must have spent hours on the phone.

"Waiting to take you down the aisle," Dad told Reba as she came up the steps to greet him, with tears in her eyes.

"Oh, Dad!"

"So happy for all three of you. Who knew, last summer, when we first talked about selling, that it would turn out like this. Your mother and I couldn't have asked for anything better."

Mom and Lucas's parents went ahead to take their places in the church, and then Carla appeared, smiling and a little nervous, practically wringing her hands. "I know you said you wanted it simple, guys," she said, "But it, um, didn't turn out that way. I've booked out the steakhouse for a special meal later, and— Are you going to bite my head off, Reba?"

Reba laughed again. "Let me think about that for a moment."

"You have to *think* about it?"

"Don't want to just let my emotions carry me away…"

Lucas broke into a grin beside her.

"…gotta be rational about this kind of thing, you see," she continued, sounding very earnest about it. "Biting your head off could turn out to be the right option, after a proper analysis of the situation."

"R-Reba?"

"But I've decided to hug you instead, you Bad Friend, trying so hard to make me happy like this! And succeeding, too."

They hugged, with Maggie squeezed gently in between and Lucas looking on, still grinning. His gaze met Reba's and she started to melt as she always did when they were close. As she always would, she knew, for the rest of her life.

He brushed her face with his cupped hand, and together they looked down at their daughter, who was fast asleep.

"Think we're all ready for this, little girl?" Reba whispered. Maggie's peaceful expression suggested that she was. "Lucas, if you want me to come down the aisle toward you, it might be time for you to get ahead of me, now."

"If I can manage to let you go," he whispered back.

"It won't be for long, and afterward you're going to have a hard time letting me go again, ever."

"Here goes, then."

He squeezed her hand and disappeared into the church. A minute later, the music of the organ swelled, signaling the start of Reba's journey toward her future, and she walked up the aisle to where Lucas was waiting for her and smiling at her with their beloved daughter's happy eyes.

* * * * *

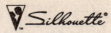

SPECIAL EDITION™

Don't miss the exciting conclusion of
The Fortunes of Texas: Reunion
three-book continuity
in Silhouette Special Edition

IN A TEXAS MINUTE
by Stella Bagwell

Available April 2005
Silhouette Special Edition #1677

When Sierra Mendoza was left with an abandoned
baby, she turned to her closest friend and confidant,
Alex Calloway. While taking care of the infant,
Sierra and Alex's relationship went from platonic
to passionate. But would deep-seated scars from Alex's
past prevent them from becoming a ready-made family?

THE
FORTUNES
OF TEXAS™:
Reunion

The price of privilege. The power of family.

Available at your favorite retail outlet.

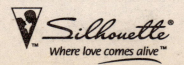

Where love comes alive™

SILHOUETTE *Romance*®

presents a ***sassy*** new romance
by Angie Ray
THE MILLIONAIRE'S REWARD
(Silhouette Romance #1764)

Wealthy tycoon Garek Wisnewski is used to
getting what he wants…and he wants new
employee Ellie Hernandez. Garek knows that
the spirited beauty is against mixing business
with pleasure, but this corporate bad boy has a
romantic merger planned, and he won't
let anything—even Ellie's halfhearted
objections—stand in his way.

*Available April 2005
at your favorite retail outlet.*

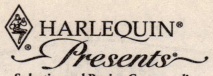